BILL GRANGER

LEAGUE OF TERROR

WARNER BOOKS

A Time Warner Company

WARNER BOOKS EDITION

Copyright © 1990 by Granger and Granger Inc.
All rights reserved.

Cover design by Gerald Pfeiffer
Cover illustration by Miles Sprinzen

Warner Books, Inc.
666 Fifth Avenue
New York, N.Y. 10103

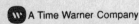 A Time Warner Company

Printed in the United States of America

This book was originally published in hardcover by Warner Books.
First Printed in Paperback: November, 1991

10 9 8 7 6 5 4 3 2 1

This is for Milt Rosenberg
and John Coyne

AUTHOR'S NOTE

The long Iran-Iraq war produced many evil side effects, not the least of which was reintroduction of nerve gas as a routine weapon in battle. Long after intelligence agencies determined Iraq was "equalizing" the war by using nerve gas against its numerically superior foe, gas continued to be dispatched in battle. Arab sympathizers with Iraq—faced with a similar problem of numerical inferiority in future wars—became intensely interested in acquiring the means of producing nerve gas. After the war, Libya—using West German technology and assistance—assembled a production facility to produce mustard gas. It was partially destroyed by sabotage in March 1990. Though use of lethal gas in warfare is proscribed by the Geneva conventions and subsequent protocols, both the United States and the Soviet Union continue to manufacture and stockpile nerve gas whose only use can be as weapons of war. There is evidence that nerve gas was used by the Soviet Union in Afghanistan.

Terrorism for profit is not a new idea—witness the success of extortion by the Black Hand societies and the Sicilian Mafia in the early part of the century. But a

AUTHOR'S NOTE

new, non-ideological terrorism—using new weapons—
has risen, threatening the machinery of business, not
the specific harm of individuals.

This book reflects these realities.

CAST OF
MAJOR CHARACTERS

Devereaux—code named "November" is the cold, primed-to-kill agent of R Section.

Rita Macklin—a tough, sexy journalist whose only flaw is that she loves the November man.

Hanley—director of operations for R Section, a bureaucrat to his fingertips and an employer who can't be trusted.

Lydia Neumann—head of R Section who knows too many secrets to not feel the burden of them.

Mac—Rita's boss, a news magazine editor who feels his career—and life—are ending too soon.

Henry McGee—self-described as "the worst man in the world," he is a terrorist-for-profit.

"Marie Dreiser"—a Berlin waif and survivor who is used by McGee—and uses him in return. "Marie" may not be her name at all.

Maureen Kilkenny—a fiery red-haired IRA revolutionary who kills better than any man.

Matthew O'Day—the IRA cell leader who is targeted for terror himself.

CAST OF CHARACTERS

Dr. Krueger—a neurologist who uses narcotics to enslave Rita Macklin.

Trevor Armstrong—vain, ruthless boss of Euro-American Airlines who has hocked his soul and now faces the bill for terror.

Dwyer—Armstrong's right-hand man who knows how to use a "horse-killer."

Juno—a man who sells death in a used vodka bottle.

My object all sublime
I shall achieve in time—
To let the punishment
Fit the crime. . . .

W. S. GILBERT

Was blind, but now I see.

"Amazing Grace"

ONE

R ita Macklin buttoned her blouse and then tucked it into her skirt. She looked for a critical moment at herself in the mirror of the dressing closet off the bathroom. The blouse was green satin and it complemented her green eyes. She wore her red hair long, as always, and her bangs swept her pale forehead. The bridge of freckles was lesser now because it was fall and she did not have as much time to spend outdoors. She ran every other day but that was early in the morning, before the sun had any power.

She put on a pale lipstick and pressed her lips and regarded the effect of the makeup.

She had not seen Devereaux for a year.

She had called him at the Section more than once and they assured her they had patched her calls through to his apartment. They couldn't say where until the night she guessed

1

New York and an inexperienced dispatcher confirmed it. But that was all—how did you find a hidden man in the labyrinth of the city? She had even asked once—"Where in New York?" But they would not tell her because the apartment was a safe house and, therefore, was secret. Everything was secret, even his existence. She was outside the shell and could not penetrate it.

She thought about him most in the mornings, like now, when she dressed in the apartment off Old Georgetown Road in Bethesda.

Her apartment complex was scarcely a mile from Bethesda Naval Hospital, and the area had been built up chaotically in the past ten years, from the time she had first come to Washington as a reporter. That depressed her, to think of how much change she had witnessed in her surroundings in what she still considered a short life here. Most of the time, she felt she was still new in the capital; and the rare times she admitted her age to herself, she got a little drunk with friends.

She was thirty-six years old. Her eyes, however bright, told her that. She had welcomed the current fashion to wear eye makeup during the day though she would not have done so if she had been younger. Even before she had known Devereaux.

She paused in the act of dressing and thought of him. The thought was dangerous at a vulnerable time like this, the first thing in the morning. It might stay with her all day.

Devereaux would have stood in the dressing foyer and watched her. He wouldn't have said anything but he would have smiled at her if she caught him watching her. The smile would have been shy, the merest trace reflecting the pleasure she gave him. It was such a simple ritual they had shared, like all their rituals.

She would have felt comfortable, as though he were complimenting her or making an act of love. He really had loved her and never said it to her. That too was part of the ritual, because words were used for lies in Devereaux's canon, and what was true must be silent. He had really loved her in all those silences they shared.

At least she thought that when she remembered him.

They had parted reluctantly more than a year ago because she really had to make him understand she couldn't tolerate life as—she wasn't even his wife, just his lover—as the lover of a case officer. Case officer. What a mundane term to describe what he really was, an intelligence agent with R Section. Not a clerk deciphering codes in a safe bureaucracy but an agent in the field, one of the tacks on a map of the world that signified operations both legal and black.

He had all the secrets dangerously stored inside him. The secrets made him a silent watcher, even if he was merely watching her dress in the little closet of her apartment. When you have secrets, even those that are dead and buried deep in memory's backyard, you cannot speak because each word must be a lie or the secrets are revealed. Lies become habit. She couldn't tolerate his life because the secrets he carried around in him put him apart from her all the time and because she knew he put himself in harm's way too often. She loved him too much to lose him; so, she had left him.

She folded her arms and hugged herself to stop from thinking about the way he had held her—sometimes in the morning like this, held her a moment before she had to leave—as though he wanted an impression of her to carry around with him during the time they were apart.

He had risen behind her on those mornings and had come to her at the mirror and placed his arms over her, to squeeze her waist, to touch her breasts, to nuzzle her neck so that he could smell her perfume as he tasted her.

Damn him.

Rita had been very sure about leaving Devereaux at the time. The doubts came a moment later. She held them off for a while, for a long while, and then she could not end her addiction to him at all. She had to call him, wherever he was. She had to at least hear the sound of his voice again, a potent placebo against the doubts and melancholy of life apart from him.

He never answered her calls.

There was only a single number and she knew it was one of the twenty-four hour answering rooms kept by R Section. She said his name and told them her code name. Her code name—though she wasn't part of Section at all, she had a code name, as he did. They would patch her through to wherever he was in time—they wouldn't tell her where he was.

There was a phone recording machine hooked up in a safe house in New York and it wasn't even his voice but a computer-generated one: "Leave a message at the tone." And then a tone, and she would tell the emptiness: "Call me."

He had not called her.

He had not come back to her. She felt relieved sometimes at that because it wasn't any good between them, not in the long run. Not as long as he was the reluctant spy for R Section, kept in harness because they needed him and they knew how to control him. He had tried once to break free with her and it had nearly cost both of them their lives. In the real world, you're on one side or the other; those are the rules.

She said those things to console herself because it was truly broken between them. He would not call her.

"Call me," she would say in the darkest moment to the sound of a beep on a recording machine. She wouldn't say more than that.

It should have been enough for him.

TWO

S he stepped out into the bright October light. The sunlight was fragmented against the golden maples behind the apartment complex. It was dazzlingly beautiful in that moment.

Rita Macklin stepped onto the new gravel on the lot, stopped, smiled at the sky and trees. The bad thoughts about Devereaux had left her; she would be all right for the rest of the day. Now she was herself, an attractive woman with merry eyes and an eager manner that pleased all men and not a few women. She could not be given to melancholy on a perfect autumn morning.

She fumbled for her car keys in her purse and pulled them out. The car was a five-year-old Ford Escort, a minimal sort of car that fitted her life and style. She hadn't wanted a car at all but her bosses insisted she have one. There are stories outside the District, Mac would say; you have to fly out of Dulles, another would say, and it would be more economical. Inside the District, she still used the clean, swift Metro underground and the poke-along buses. Sometimes she would just walk all the way home, up Massachusetts to Wisconsin Avenue and out to the Old Georgetown Road, marveling at all that was new in the city, comforted by all the things that had not changed. But today she had to go to Dulles, so she would use the car.

She had her keys in hand as she reached the car. In the next moment, she was on the ground.

She had fallen, she thought.

She felt a dull sickness in her stomach and wondered if she had broken the heel of her right shoe. The shoes cost $125, which was obscene, but she had loved them when she saw them in the store on L Street.

She thought her skirt would be soiled by the gravel and dirt in the parking lot. A stupid fall and she had ruined her clothes and would have to change and miss the next flight . . . The thoughts came jumbled and fast as she lay on the gravel and tried to decide why she felt sick. She tried to turn on her hip and push herself up but her right arm didn't work. She thought she had sprained it in falling. And why had she fallen?

Then she felt the pain from her belly up across the right side of her chest to her shoulder and from her shoulder down to her right elbow. The pain was centered in her right side but she couldn't understand why she wanted to retch.

Instead, Rita moaned. And blood filled her mouth and her nose, although she did not know this yet.

She blinked to be able to see better. She saw a man coming

between the rows of parked cars. The sun was behind him and he was merely a shadow until he came near. He carried a briefcase. She noticed the initials on the briefcase and thought it was pretentious to have initials on your case. She wouldn't have thought of doing that. She counted herself a simple person. She wouldn't have owned a car but she had to go to Dulles where the plane would have left already—

Oh my God, she thought, I'm going to scream in a moment.

It was the lawyer who lived in the apartment at the other end of the hall. Tom. Tom something, they had met at a party of a mutual friend in the same apartment building. He had wanted to put the hit on her but he really wasn't her type at all. Now she was lying here, embarrassing herself, embarrassing him. What an awful way to start a—

She moaned again and saw that frightened look in his eyes, as though he were looking at something quite horrible. His look frightened her more than being on the ground.

"Please," she said.

"My God, Rita, your blouse, your face—"

She wasn't seeing him very well.

What about her blouse?

"You're bleeding, you've been shot," Tom said. "My God, Rita, I'll call emergency . . . I heard the shot."

What about her blouse? There was nothing wrong with her blouse. She looked down at her blouse and saw that the green satin was wet on the right side and that the green had turned a much darker color. What about her blouse?

He was leaving her and the world spun around so that the rows of cars narrowed around her. Were they going to crush her? What did she care? She didn't want to close her eyes because she thought she might fall asleep right there, between the parked cars in the parking lot. That would make her look foolish. Tom what's-his-name certainly shouldn't have left her to look foolish. Was she drunk? She had gone running five miles this morning, all the way out to the Beltway and back, and she had eaten an English muffin, Lite cream cheese, and a tomato slice for breakfast . . .

She closed her eyes despite herself.

THREE

Devereaux picked up the telephone in the living room of the three-room safe "house" on West Fifty-eighth Street in Manhattan.

He was just over six feet tall, with graying hair and absolutely pewter eyes. For a moment, he only listened to the complex whine of the scrambler becoming activated.

"November," Hanley said.

"Control," Devereaux responded.

"There's been . . . a rather bad thing," Hanley said. His voice was so unusually delicate, almost hesitant. It was the voice of someone trying to be a friend while conveying both sympathy and bad news.

What a peculiar tone of voice. Hanley was only control and not his friend by any means.

"Rita Macklin was shot this morning in the parking lot of

her apartment building,'' Hanley said. "We were only notified a little while ago, through the editor of that magazine she worked for. She had left her building at the usual time, according to him; she was catching a flight to Phoenix.''

Devereaux waited. If he spoke now, he would betray himself to Hanley. He thought of the voice on the answering machine and how he had been tempted to call her and catch the shuttle back to her. But he had not because it would have been no good again. They had loved each other too much to put up with hurts and disappointments in his work for Section. He understood how much he hurt her, and there was no way not to go on hurting her. So he had cut it off, finally, even if she could not. He always dreaded returning to this apartment, dreaded the blinking red light on the answering machine that meant someone had called. Would it be her voice? "Call me.'' But he loved her too much to do that.

"Goddamn you, Hanley, is she dead?''

"She's in surgery. She lost a lot of blood before they got to her. She was in shock at the scene; her eyes were rolling back above her lids.'' He paused; the graphic description chilled both of them. There was a long silence before Devereaux spoke.

"Who shot her?''

"An assassin,'' Hanley said. "Shot from a grove of maples behind her apartment house. She wasn't robbed, she was set up to be shot.''

"Who shot her?'' Devereaux said.

"The police say they don't have any clues, that—''

"Screw the police. Screw the goddamn police.'' Just this close to losing control. They both understood it. More silence, more waiting. The telephone line buzzed faintly. Devereaux pinched the bridge of his nose and closed his eyes. "I want to know who shot her."

"Devereaux," Hanley said. "I don't know. We're working on it through liaisons. With the Bureau. We're doing what we can—"

"Where is she?"

"Saint Margaret's Hospital. We made certain she had the best. Has. The doctor has a good reputation, but she was in shock and the loss of blood . . . Also a concussion when she fell. After she was hit. That concerned him greatly for a time. They took X rays, a C-Scan, EEG . . ." The medical terms were supposed to soothe; they did not. "Everything is being done . . ."

Devereaux again made a silence by not propping up the dying words of Hanley's monologue. He looked out the single living room window at the hurly-burly below. Eighth Avenue was in full early-evening swing. The streets were crowded with commuters and idlers, ladies of the evening and boys of the night, theatergoers and tired young women walking home from work in limp gray suits and tennis shoes. The city had worked desperately hard all day and now it would play desperately hard all night. There was no respite from the sense of desperation, even in the nightmares of sleep.

Devereaux saw Rita as she was the first time, on that beach in Florida a long time ago when he only meant to use her and not to love her. *Call me.* He could have picked up the phone yesterday or the day before or a year before.

"What was she working on?" He tried a calm tone in the face of the nightmare. A fire engine wailed beyond his windows, one more scream in the night.

"A piece about the renaissance in city life in Pittsburgh.

Also this story in Phoenix, about the crime syndicate. It was about the reporter who was killed there years ago. Don Bolles, blown up in his car," Hanley said. "Her editor, Mac-Cormick, he told me that. He didn't seem surprised that I had called him. I told him I was with the Bureau but I knew he didn't believe me. He knew about you, about her . . . relationship to you."

"That was past," Devereaux said.

"But he knew I wasn't FBI," Hanley said.

"What else was she working on?"

"Nothing of importance, nothing to get shot over. It was the anniversary of his death, this Bolles fellow, it was a retrospective and a look at the city today. I don't really understand journalists but he told me it was routine."

"Is he sure? Who has her notes on the Outfit?"

"I beg your pardon?"

Devereaux closed his eyes and pinched the bridge of his nose.

"The crime syndicate in Phoenix. Did he have her notes?"

"No."

"Then why—"

"I notified the Bureau, I told you. They're looking into it."

"Yes. You told me."

More silence.

"Are you coming to Washington?"

"Yes," Devereaux said.

"We can send a man to the airport to meet you. Drive you to the hospital. You can have a car at your disposal."

"Yes." He said it in a dull voice, keeping the conversation from flickering into silence now because he was suddenly afraid of silence, afraid he would hear her voice.

The apartment was dark. He had been sitting in the dark, drinking vodka, listening to the roar of the city outside his windows. He had not thought about Rita Macklin for days and he had wondered if he would eventually reach the point when he would not think about her at all. Memory can be contained and all old wounds turned to healed scars by new experience. It wasn't the passage of time at all that did it but burying the past under each new, unrelated experience. Now she was back in all his thoughts, she was all old wounds torn open again.

"There's been a lot of this. Murder. In the capital. The police think it was unrelated to her, perhaps—"

"Don't tell me that. Not in Bethesda, not in the morning. That's bullshit, Hanley."

"You're upset. You have every reason to be. I called you as soon as I was told . . ."

Hanley's voice craved sympathy. He wanted Devereaux to be glad that he had acted so humanely. He wanted Devereaux's forgiveness for whatever it was he had ever done.

Devereaux replaced the receiver.

He walked into the bedroom and turned on the small brass lamp at the side of his bed. He rarely slept in the bed but on the couch, under a single prickly wool blanket, generally falling asleep while he read a book. The apartment was littered with books. They were stacked on the floor everywhere because the safe house had no bookshelves, although it contained two television sets. The books made some mark of his on the place. And he kept vodka in the refrigerator, neat rows of bottles of vodka so that he would never be without it.

He placed the 9mm Beretta in the bag with a few bits of clothing. And the blue passport. And the British passport too, in case he would have to become someone else. He slipped the money pouch—Velcro close, waterproof—inside his waistband.

He zipped the canvas bag and turned toward the door. The front entry had four locks. He opened the door, stepped into the tiled hall, and closed the door. He relocked all four locks, sending the dead bolts home four times, four thuds of metal against metal in the silent chamber of the hall. The door was solid steel and so was the framing around the door.

He walked to the elevator cage and pressed the button. The machinery pulled the elevator slowly to the sixth level.

"*Call me*," she had said on the message tape. He had wanted to purge her from his life.

The doors opened and he stepped inside the cage.

Call me.

He wanted tears in that moment but none came. He listened to her voice over and over as the cage descended.

FOUR

Devereaux sat in the lounge on the second floor. The hospital was full of night sounds, groans from the darkened halls and television sets. All the fear of sickness and death in a hospital is concentrated in the night corridors and is endured through the narcotics of conversation and banal TV entertainment, punctuated by groans.

He was alone. He didn't need the driver or the car. Or goddamned Section and the goddamned sympathy of someone like Hanley. Section had tied him to remain an agent—to abandon Rita—because they knew all the secret things that Devereaux had done. They had Devereaux tied forever to them because they needed him. Goddamned Section. For one moment a long time ago, he had traded his soul for something Section knew he wanted to have. Thought he needed—until he met Rita Macklin.

Section. He felt hate and he didn't know if it was for himself or Section, but Section was sitting out there and he could kick at it, maybe bring it down, shoot to kill . . .

She was dying. He felt it. Dying was pure cold, pure white.

"Mr. Devereaux?"

He looked at the surgeon and was shocked to see how young he was. Or was it merely that Devereaux was growing old?

"Your friend is out of surgery now," the surgeon said. He had changed his smock because of the blood on it. For a surgeon, he had learned sensitivity somewhere.

Devereaux waited. He almost never asked questions because the silence makes a better questioner.

"She's in guarded condition." He waited for a question but none came.

Devereaux sat, staring at him, not with curiosity or hostility or any emotion on his face.

"There was a lot of damage. She's lost part of her right lung. That's what took so long. There was no way to save all of it. When the bullet entered, it exploded. Fortunately for her life, the bullet was not dead-on. It entered below her right breast but exited sharply up, through her shoulder. The shoulder muscles were damaged; I don't know how great the neurological damage is. While she was under, I tried to get a grasping response from her right hand but she couldn't manage it. But this can be temporary. I mean, the partial paralysis."

He was telling Devereaux everything, as calmly as possible. Devereaux's silence demanded everything.

"The point is, she has a healthy heart, she has good circulation, she was undoubtedly athletic. These are the pluses. The lung. Well, you can live with one lung, let alone only losing part of one . . . but the trauma of losing it this way and the loss of blood before surgery count against. I'm trying to be as honest as I can.''

Devereaux knew dying was cold, was white. It was still there and he could sense it. "Is she going to die?"

"I don't know. I hope not."

Devereaux got up. He saw the surgeon was shorter than he was and that his eyes were very tired. "Is there anything anyone can do?"

"She's being monitored, I'm on call . . . there's nothing to do now."

"Can I see her?"

"There's . . . look, Mr. Devereaux. Her head is bandaged. From the concussion. There's a lot of healing going on right now, tubes, a sling. I really wish you wouldn't.''

Devereaux saw her anyway, from the door of the bright-lit room where she lay. Her eyes were closed and her beautiful red hair was capped by a crown of bandages. He saw the machines that measured the course of her life and the green lines that noted she had advanced another heartbeat.

"Oh, goddamn it," Devereaux said. He let the door close without a sound.

FIVE

Room 803 of the Dupont Plaza Hotel was small and marginally clean. The window overlooked the neighborhood around the Circle. It was just after one in the morning. The city looked seedy and dark at night because of the overgrowth of southern trees on small northern lots and the dangerous shadows of streetlamps obscured by the trees. The usual derelicts occupied the park in the middle of Dupont Circle.

It was just after one in the morning and they had given him a bottle of vodka at the liquor store on Wisconsin in Bethesda. In the empty lobby of the hotel, he had dropped a ten-dollar bill on the counter to order a bucket of ice and a large glass brought to his room. The clerk explained that the bar was closed and there was an ice machine on each floor and that the plastic glasses in the room would have to suffice. Even money could not buy service.

Devereaux began to feel all the aches of all the wounds he had received over the years, physical and psychic. The clerk at the front desk watched him limp to the elevator bank and press the button and wait. The clerk thought the gray man must be ill and he hoped he wouldn't die in his room on his shift.

Devereaux would not sleep. He fetched a bucket of ice from the buzzing machine in the alcove down the hall and brought it back to his room. He unwrapped a plastic glass and filled it with ice and vodka and went to the chair by the window and sat down.

For a long time, he sat at the window and stared out at the darkness, a palpable darkness under the orange glow of the streetlamps. Anticrime lights, installed long before the city understood what crime it would have.

They called the capital Murder City now. Anarchy was the rule of law. The Ellipse and the Mall were the same as ever, surrounded by trees and grassy fields and federal buildings of classical splendor and open tour buses full of kids. But beyond, on the narrow neighborhood streets, drug dealers killed each other at the drop of a bag of crack. Drug dealers killed each other and those in between. The trail of drugs reached across the capital into the suburbs. Everyone, it seemed, was drunk or drugged or about to be made a victim.

The Bethesda police detective at the hospital wanted to know if Miss Macklin was into drugs. Devereaux had stared through him for a moment until he repeated his question. Devereaux had turned without a reply and started down the corridor. "I asked you a question," the detective had said.

Devereaux had said, "I answered it."

He closed his eyes because he was tired and because he wanted to think about what Rita had been doing, the story about the Outfit in Phoenix. He had to think of concrete things, of reasons to assassinate her, or he could not endure any of the pain. He did not know how to grieve a loss because he had burned out that process from his soul. The vodka was cold and warmed him. He would get a little drunk but he knew he would not sleep until Rita finally recovered or died. And if she died, he thought he would kill the man who hurt her and then he would kill himself quickly and not slowly, the way he was doing it with the alcohol.

He was very close to being out of control and part of him knew it.

He kept himself under a strict control all the time, but every now and then the sheet of calm was cracked and the shards of shattered glass in his soul made him a dangerous beast who does not reason but acts through instinct. Before that, though, before he killed the person who shot Rita Macklin, he would have to find him.

So he needed control.

He opened his eyes. Suddenly, he slammed his fist against the plasterboard wall. He dented it. Pain shot into his wrist. He did it again to feel the pain.

There. It was ebbing. The beast in him growled reluctantly but slunk away into his belly, away from his heart.

He put down the glass of vodka to pick up the ringing telephone.

He held the receiver next to his ear. The voice was familiar and he understood everything in that moment.

"Hello, Dev," Henry McGee said. As close as the next room. The voice was couched in country accents and belonged to the worst man on earth.

Devereaux waited. His hand stung.

"I shot her. This morning. She gonna make it?"

Never answer.

"It wasn't nothin' about her, except she had this connection to you. Remember, I knew about that. So when it comes time to settlin' scores, I figure the best is to let you hurt a little. I mean, before I kill you. I'm gonna kill you, you know."

Devereaux said nothing.

"Now, it could of been that she was just a piece of tail for you and you might have felt passing bad about her gettin' shot, but I sort of guessed it was more than that. You been real good stayin' away from her but that's all right, you're in D.C. now so I know I scored."

"You going to talk me to death?"

Henry chuckled. "Honest to God, I hardly ever do anything except for money unless it's a pussy to pass the time but I figured I owed you for the two years in that shithouse in P.A. Also, for gettin' my trail dirty with the Soviets so I can't go back to Mother Moscow. I owed you for a lot, Dev, and now I'm paying back. Didn't you figure I was gonna pay you what I owed you?"

"You've been seeing too many old gangster movies."

Silence.

"Tell me it don't hurt, Dev."

Devereaux said nothing.

"I wanted to wound her, not kill her, but what the hell, you can't always get what you want."

Devereaux closed his eyes. Was she dead?

"But I called the hospital, they say she's in 'guarded' condition. Fucking hospitals can't talk English no more. Means they put a guard on you or what?"

"When do you want me to kill you?" Devereaux said.

"There. I see I scored hard, didn't I? Well, Dev, it's this

way. I shot your girlie and I'm comin' after you now, but it won't be a shootout at high noon, I can tell you. I been getting smarts up about how to do things and there's money in it. So when I come to kill you, you'll be so surprised there for about one second before you die. It'll be like that. Meantime, just think about your piece of tail in the hospital, all fucked up by your old friend, Henry McGee.''

The connection was broken.

The beast roared out of his skin and filled the room with its growls and rumbles.

Devereaux did not make a sound. His eyes glittered, even in the dim light. He took the 9mm Beretta out of the bag and checked the clip and put the pistol into his belt holster.

He picked up the telephone and called the operator of the hotel.

"That call was placed from the lobby, sir," the operator said.

That close. He took the automatic out of his belt and unsnapped the safety.

He walked out of the room to the elevator bank and waited, pacing up and down before the row of closed doors.

Then the middle door opened and he entered the cage and pressed "L."

The beast scarcely breathed. His breath was very deep, very slow, yet as sensitive as the adrenaline that alerted every muscle and nerve.

He stepped into the lobby and it was empty. The bar off the lobby was closed. The restaurant was locked and in darkness.

He went to the front desk.

Yes, they had noticed a man calling his room. A dark-haired man, they thought. No, he had gone out the Connecticut Avenue entrance a few moments ago.

The streets were nearly empty. A beggar slept in the doorway of an Italian restaurant across the way. Devereaux slowly panned the street and then walked to the corner. The side streets were in twilight, orange and leafy from trees and streetlamps.

He saw a man on the next corner and started for him. Ten feet away, he said, "Henry."

The man turned. He was the same height and build but that was all. "Whaddaya want?"

Devereaux did not reply. He turned down the block and completed the circle back to his hotel, entering from the side street.

There was only one clerk on duty in the lobby, not the same as a moment before.

"Has anyone come in just now?"

The clerk looked up from the *Post*. "Are you a guest, sir?"

"Yes. I'm a guest." He showed the key with the large square top embossed with his room number. "Did anyone come in, in just the last few minutes?"

"Another guest," the clerk said. He was trying to be annoyed, as though he had other things to do.

"What did he look like?"

"I didn't take a look."

"Did he have a key?"

"He had a key," the clerk said.

"A dark-haired man," Devereaux said.

"I couldn't say, sir."

Devereaux went to the three-door elevator bank and pressed a button. A cage opened for him a moment later. Once the door closed, he pulled the pistol again and cocked it. He held the pistol out from his body and turned slightly, to present a smaller profile.

The door opened at the floor above his floor without a sound. He got off and waited for the door to close behind him. An exit sign glowed feebly at the far end. The hotel was shaped like a V with the point facing Dupont Circle. His room was on the southwest side of the V.

Devereaux went to the stairs and opened the stairwell door. He moved to the concrete stairs and then removed his shoes. He stepped in stocking feet down the stairs, the pistol scanning the next flight at the landing a moment before he peered over.

He held his breath. Henry McGee was very good, and Devereaux had drunk vodka and thoughts of Rita Macklin were pushing clear judgment into emotion. He knew all this and he was very cautious.

He opened the stairwell door at his own floor and waited and then stepped into the corridor. It was empty.

He edged along the gray wall to the point of the V and looked around. Silence. Corridors with littered trays set before some doors. Not a sound but the hum of the building that trembled with the suppressed noise of fans from the cooling and heating plant.

He held the pistol in his right hand and the key in his left.

He unlocked his door and pushed it with his foot. The room was as he had left it, in darkness. He fumbled for the switch on the wall by the door.

He turned the lights on.

The force of the explosion drove him headfirst across the hall into the door opposite. He hit the door with his head and left shoulder and then the rest of his back. The explosion blew the door of his room from its hinges and splattered shards of wood into the man momentarily impaled on the door opposite. The shards of wood tattooed his face and body, driving through his clothes into his flesh.

For a second, Devereaux knew exactly what had happened and how Henry had killed him.

SIX

$\mathbf{H}$anley was more tired than he could remember. He sat in the red leather chair in Mrs. Neumann's corner office in the Department of Agriculture Building. The offices of R Section were located on a floor of the neoclassical building that—officially—did not exist. Mrs. Neumann, director of R Section, stood at the window and looked down the length of Fourteenth Street. Traffic from the bridge was piled against the gridlock of central Washington. It was 8:14 in the morning and the report from the District of Columbia police as well as the Federal Bureau of Investigation summary was on her desk. Hanley had brought the two agencies in and lied to them about the nature of Devereaux's employment. It was enough to tell them that Devereaux was important enough for them to find his attackers.

"Do you have any word?" she rasped. Her voice was always harsh and direct.

Hanley had been called by Tomkins of the FBI at 3:30 A.M. The police had found the gray, unmarked credit card in Devereaux's clothes and notified the FBI. The FBI knew the card was the ID of agents of R Section.

"Nothing. His skull was fractured, his left arm and shoulder were hurt but no broken bones, he suffered extensive lacerations." Hanley shook his head. "First Miss Macklin and now him. In less than twenty-four hours. This is beyond belief."

Mrs. Neumann said nothing. She now contemplated the Mall and the 505-foot obelisk on the Ellipse that is Washington's memorial.

"Did you explain the connection to them?"

"Miss Macklin and Devereaux? Of course not."

"But we know there must be a connection."

"No matter what, this matter has to be contained. My God, they'd love it on the Hill to know that one of our classified men was dating a journalist."

"But not for some time," Mrs. Neumann said. She probed directly. "And why not for some time? And why would they be killed now? Some delayed reaction from Moscow Center?"

"I don't know," Hanley said. She could ask a hundred questions and he wouldn't know. He shook his head again. It was not a characteristic gesture.

"Can't we do anything?"

"The Bureau has charter in the United States. We do not."

"Damnit, Hanley, we've broken rules before."

That was so unlike her that Hanley registered surprise a moment before frowning. "He wasn't assigned, nothing was pending. Nothing involved Miss Macklin. Maybe it was co-incidence."

Mrs. Neumann didn't comment.

"Even if he survives, he's finished. They as much as said that when I first called emergency. They're not even certain they can save his right leg, and if they can, they're not certain that he won't be paralyzed. He broke his neck, Mrs. Neumann."

"They're not certain how serious the break is. A chip. Breaking your neck is a layman's term," she said. She was clutching and Hanley knew it.

"And I'm a layman and he broke his neck," Hanley said again.

She knew. She had called as well, before Hanley made his report. She knew and Hanley had to repeat the words to try to put them in perspective.

Agents died on duty. Not as often as one might think but they died in action. Or they disappeared. Networks were blown and agents with fanciful file names like Beethoven and January and Lion were suddenly stricken from active duty and presumed dead. Or lost to Moscow Center. Even in the age of *glasnost*, the war remained.

But this agent was Devereaux and Mrs. Neumann knew him and Hanley had been his control. In the 201 file, he was identified as November. The code name suited him. He had been morose and difficult and contrary at times, questioning the bureaucracy of Section in all his actions. But he had seemed very indestructible to Mrs. Neumann.

Had seemed. Had been. Was he really past?

She shook her head to rid herself of the thought and then crossed the spartan office to her desk. She picked up the FBI dossier. "Semcon was used and a simple electric prime hooked to the wall switch. He entered the room, turned on the lights and was blown up. The materials smell of Libya, Iraq, in that neighborhood.''

"All Middle East stations are alerted and the reports are starting to come in. I've destroyed the budget on this one," Hanley said. "Our network in Tripoli is more difficult to contact. The stationmaster at Naples is trying to make a connection with them.''

"Who is Naples?''

"New man. Echo. Do you want his two-oh-one file?"

"No.'' She put the file down. "Miss Macklin was doing a story on the crime syndicate . . .''

"What on earth would the connection be to November?"

"Perhaps they thought she was a government agent—''

"The syndicate does not pick fights with federal agents. Or journalists, for that matter.''

"Except for the man killed in Phoenix,'' she said.

"That was a long time ago,'' Hanley said. He studied the tent of his fingers. "Everything was a long time ago.'' He looked up. "It has nothing to do with us, with Section—''

"The government mixes itself up at times. Why not the crime syndicate?'' Said with weariness or hope. Everyone needs an answer sometimes. Straws were grasped.

"What are we going to do?'' she said after a moment.

Hanley was prepared. He began to speak about alerting the network liaison with the Israeli Mossad and Mrs. Neumann held up her hand to interrupt.

"About Devereaux.''

Hanley blinked.

"He broke his neck, man,'' Mrs. Neumann said. "Probably paralyzed. If he survives. A piece of wood a half inch thick pierced his lung. He isn't coming back. What are we going to do if he does? I mean, what can we expect to ask him to do?''

It was the difference between them. Hanley saw it without bitterness. In length of service, he should have been named director of Section. Instead, he was still director of operations, still old control to the first tier of agents. Hanley was tactics, Mrs. Neumann was strategy. She would let Hanley take care of the chase for Devereaux's assassin. What about after? If he recovered? With his bag of secrets firmly in memory? What would they do for him then? The British had made a bad habit of cheaping out old agents and controls and it had come back to haunt them more than once, like the man in Australia who had revealed all his British intelligence secrets in the bitterness of his impoverished retirement. Devereaux must not be allowed to be bitter. Section would do the right thing.

Hanley admired such foresightedness.

"Yes." He almost smiled. "A solid pension, solid disability payment. He's earned it."

Mrs. Neumann seemed surprised. It wasn't the answer she wanted at all.

"No. I mean . . . inside. For him to come in, become an inside man."

Hanley let his smile fade. "I don't know, Mrs. Neumann."

"What's wrong with it?"

"Mrs. Neumann. November is difficult. A good man but difficult. Not a team player. We need team players. In the . . . central office. He could disrupt . . ."

Mrs. Neumann let him stutter off into silence. It wasn't Hanley's fault either. The square peg and round hole were not met.

"Disability."

"He tried to retire once. There was a wet contract on him."

"He did," she admitted.

"He needed us. Then. And we needed him. He's been around a long time."

"A pension. A disability." Repeating words like automatic prayers. "The best thing."

"If he survives."

But she didn't want to think of the other possibility.

SEVEN

"**W**here were you?"

"All over," Henry McGee said. He touched her face with what passed for affection in him. She had cleaned up nice and he wasn't ashamed of showing her. There was grit in the girl, too, and he could use that. He had someone do her hair and he got someone to buy her clothes. She would look good on the Champs-Elysées. A skinny girl, but skinny was always in fashion and, in a curious way, fashion counted a lot to Henry McGee. And she screwed about as well as anyone he had ever had.

Marie Dreiser—that is what she called herself most of the time—smiled at his touch. She wore the bright silk dress just for him.

They sat in the café in Rome that is less than a hundred feet up the Via Veneto from the United States embassy. Two marines were on the gates of the embassy and they looked all spit-and-polish in the warm Roman sun.

Marie Dreiser. He had met her in Berlin and stayed with her during the months he had been hiding from KGB. Henry had been set up for his old employers by Devereaux and damned Section, and they had almost got him more than once.

The irony was that Marie was a gift from Devereaux. Henry smiled every time he thought of that. She didn't know it and Devereaux didn't know it even when he was alive but it was enough that Henry knew it.

"Why are you smiling, Henry?"

"Thinking about things, honey."

"About America?"

He had been gone three weeks. Had to set things up, first for Rita, then for Devereaux. Took care of them both in one day. It would have been nice to spread it out but Devereaux was dangerous—emphasis on the *was*—and Henry had been burned by him before. Waited for her three mornings before she used the damned car and then took her down with one shot. He saw her go down and he wasn't sorry she was still alive because he might run across her sweet ass again. But Devereaux. Had to kill the sonofabitch twice to make sure he was dead. He was dead this time, all right.

The smile spread. "Just the business I had in the U.S. Worked out fine, even if it cost me some money. We gotta have some ready, honey; we're dipping into reserves."

"Will you take me to America, sometime?"

"Take you everywhere, honey," Henry said. He felt good, felt affectionate, felt like finishing his espresso and taking Marie up to the Excelsior and giving it to her all afternoon. In every way he could think of and some he hadn't thought of yet. "But now we gotta rustle up some money because I had to spend some in the States. Yes sir. Gotta spend money to make money, but now we gotta make it.''

"I can always steal. I'm a thief, a good one. Didn't I steal for you in Berlin when you were hiding?''

It had been very frightening at first, to be seeking a hideout in a strange city. To be a helpless dependent on this strange girl. She was a tough Berlin gamine who had grown up on the streets and been raped at twelve. Or so she said.

For six months, KGB had hunted him and he had survived because of Marie Dreiser in the dirty old city of Berlin that she knew so well. He had lived in two rooms beneath the elevated railroad tracks, listened to the rumble of passing trains every hour of the day, felt his claustrophobia return as it had nearly strangled him the two years he was in prison. Two years of his life, thanks to Devereaux and R Section. Two fucking years.

But Devereaux had been on Marie's trail in that business that finally led to Rome and the old cardinal in the Vatican. Devereaux had saved her life when the old priest wanted to kill her. Devereaux never knew that he had given Henry a gift by saving Marie's life. And Marie would never know it was Henry who had killed Devereaux in Washington.

Devereaux was finally dead.

Henry McGee smiled.

Saw the fire engines roll up at the hotel and then the cops and then the FBI car. They carried Devereaux's body out on a stretcher and put it in an ambulance, but that hadn't bothered Henry McGee. No one was going to survive that blast.

He couldn't tell Marie about it. She had some affection for Devereaux because he had saved her life. Just as well not to tell Marie because he had three or four more uses for her before he was set up and could get rid of her. He liked a gal with guts. Marie had stolen for him in Berlin those terrible six months of hiding. She had fed him, housed him, clothed him with her thefts. And she had gone to bed with him every time, even if the bed was the dresser or the kitchen table.

"We don't have to steal now," Henry said. He sipped his cappuccino. Life strutted along the Veneto as it did in every quarter of Rome, living in the streets, shouting from morning until past midnight, using the ancient buildings as mere props for a street opera.

"Then what do we have to do?" Marie said.

"I spent time in the States learning about what we got to do," Henry McGee said. "You read the papers, honey? You know what's going on in the world?"

"What am I supposed to know?"

"People dancing on the Berlin Wall. Hungary going queer for the West. And just this week, they had a conference in Washington District of Columbia to talk about antiterrorism. That was KGB and CIA. Imagine the day ever would come when the whole world would be putting on a happy face?"

"I'm not political, Henry," Marie said. "I know about Berlin but, believe me, nothing like that lasts."

"Terror, honey. It's all disorganized and doesn't turn a profit. There's no real point to it if it doesn't make money. Take the IRA. Been fighting in Belfast for twenty years and all they got to show for it is this ragtag rebel army, a few jobs, a few millions in arms . . . why, it hardly seems worth the trouble."

She waited. She knew Henry was only thinking out loud, not really talking to her. She understood some of it and her instincts took over on the rest of it.

"I been on both sides of politics, honey. Right now, it isn't paying very well. Not for me. You got the goddamned chief of the American armed forces touring Soviet missile facilities. The cold war has lost its Freon.''

Her eyes were closed, head tilted up. The sun felt good on her face.

''You gonna get a suntan, honey?''

''It feels good,'' she said, opening her eyes. He was smiling in his nasty way.

''You know, we ain't down here for pleasure.''

''I wondered about that.''

''This is the place to be you want certain things. Weapons. Ole Italy sticking down into the Mediterranean like a finger waiting to poke North Africa in the ass. That's why we're here. North Africa is full of nasty folks making nasty stuff for terrorism.''

''Is that right?''

''I did my research in the States. Made contacts. Met people behind the terrorists. Money people, arms dealers, all that monkey stuff. It's interesting but it's limited.''

''Do they make bombs in Africa?'' Marie said.

Henry grinned again, shook his head. ''You're closer, honey, but you ain't there yet.'' He sipped the milky coffee and licked a trace of the honey-brown liquid off his lips. Marie—hell, who even knew if that was her name but that's what she called herself most of the time—Marie was a good one, never seemed shocked by anything, but he wondered if she was just crazy enough to go along with everything.

''Honey, trouble with bombs is they don't really scare the shit out of anyone anymore. And then there's all the personnel involved. And getting the goddamned bomb through to the right target. You and I ain't got time to organize all that, train people.''

''What do you want in this part of the world?''

Henry let a smile lighten his dark features. He ignored the question. "Terror has territory. Take Britain. I like Britain as a place to set up operations. Speak the language, know the customs, all that. I just gotta get me the right target, that's what I ain't found yet. But I know who the mule is gonna be when I do find it."

"Who?"

"Some boys from the IRA. Irish Republican Army. Do any kind of terror in Britain and the first patsy you think of is the IRA. And the thing is, they're hurting now for weapons and stuff, now that Czechoslovakia is going straight and not sending them the arms like they used to. IRA is definitely what I got in mind when I find the target."

"You are going to make a new terror," Marie said in her Berlin-accented voice. She made it so simple and clear. Henry gaped at her a moment. He was truly amazed. In fact, he admired her for a second or so and that had the odd effect of arousing him. She might have just licked the inside of his ear, coming up with an answer like that.

"A new terror," he repeated. "Exactly it. I never put a name on it but that's what it is. It's going to operate in Britain and when it's over, I'll have three, four million and the Brits will have their usual suspects and you and me are home free."

Marie stared at him with her tawny eyes. She was young but there was something a hundred years old about her as well. "And what will I have?"

"Me, honey, I thought you understood that."

"You don't fool me much, Henry. And I never fool myself. I don't think you've even thought that far."

Henry McGee shook his head. "You're right. I can't fool you."

"Oh, try," she said. "I hid you in Berlin when the Russians were looking for you. I could have sold you but you knew I liked you. I get used to a man. You're good in bed, Henry.''

''And every other place we do it.'' He put his hand on her bare leg and squeezed the inside of her thigh. She closed her eyes a moment and then looked at him again.

''Are we going to kill many people?''

''Does that bother you?''

''I can kill people. I killed my father.''

''You tell me that but I think that's one of your stories. You got your stories all mixed up with dreams.''

''Maybe I just want you to think that.''

''You don't do no killing if it comes to killing. I need you, another hand, eyes-and-ears, courier, someone to handle the phone. I ain't a one-man band. When we make it, you can come with me. Or take a share, whatever you want.''

She thought about it. She tried not to let the money get in the way of her judgment. Like most people, she failed. It was a lot of money.

''I don't know,'' she said. She knew.

''Think it over.'' Henry saw he had her. ''We're being checked by certain people right now. To see who we are, to see if we are bona fides. That's why we're waiting here in the splendid capital of Italy. We might have to move just like that when the setup is made. Naples, probably, but maybe even Morocco. We just sit and wait and let them look us over.''

''Who are they?''

''People who got something I want. I told you, this is the part of Europe to be in when you're looking for new and exotic weapons.''

''What do you want? Not bombs.''

"Better than bombs. When we get our load, then we move to Dublin and start figuring on who our mules are gonna be. And all along, we got to find the target, the right target."

And he squeezed her thigh beneath her dress again and she realized it was the thought of an instrument of death that had aroused him. She didn't think she was afraid of him—she wasn't afraid of any man—but it rattled her in that moment to realize Henry McGee was sexually aroused by terror.

EIGHT

F   light 147. There were 286 people in tourist class, 19 in business class, 6 in first class.

The people in tourist class were arranged across three sections of seats. The seats were narrow enough to be uncomfortable to all but the smallest of the adults. There were sixteen children who were also uncomfortable but not because of the seats. Like all children, they had not learned the suffering patience necessary to endure the tedious hours of flight. They didn't like this at all and squirmed their little bodies this way and that to find some soothing position. Some cried, some talked, some had managed sleep in the narrow seats.

They ate a precooked dinner of underdone veal, mashed potatoes, vegetables of different colors, either lime Jell-O or lime jelly, coffee in plastic cups, and a small bit of carrot cake. There were dinner rolls and pats of butter sealed in foil.

After dinner, the movie screen at the front of the cabin showed *Halloween Heaven*, a film merging the genres of horror and romantic comedy. There were many drinks sold in small bottles, the most prevalent liquor being vodka followed by gin followed by scotch followed by Canadian blended whiskey.

The seats in business class were marginally larger but were arranged in less crowded rows. Two men in this section ignored dinner (approximately the same meal as that served in tourist but with the addition of a half bottle of very bad California wine) and worked at their laptop computers. One composed a memorandum explaining the market niche for his firm in the new Common Market of post-1992. The other composed incredibly blunt pornography, partially to combat the boredom of the transatlantic flight, partially because he thought he could show his work to the black-haired male flight attendant who showed every sign of being as gay as the computer-user.

In first class, roast beef was served on china plates of a particularly sturdy, cheap design. The roast beef was individually sliced by a man in a *toque blanche* at the front of the section. There was free champagne, which was too warm. One veteran first-class traveler was asleep, his feet encased in slippers given out by the airline in a flight survival kit that included a toothbrush, toothpaste, razor, and cologne, as though these items would not have been brought along by the first-class travelers. The name of the airline—Euro-American—was emblazoned on the side of the plastic kit containing the gratuities.

There were no children in first class and only one child in business class.

The plane followed the familiar great circle route that extends northwest from the European north coast, across Britain, almost to the tip of southern Greenland.

Those who wished looked down on the winter waves slamming the shore of Greenland. It was November and there was ice on the land and in the ocean. The plane continued to describe its arc as it now turned south and west toward the North American continent.

In the cockpit, the crew of three had finished their meals. They had all chosen the roast beef. Their trays were stacked at the back of the crowded cockpit, which was dark, the better to read the maze of gauges, lights, and computer readings. No one was actually flying the plane in the sense that a driver drives a car. The plane flew itself, and it was exactly six miles behind the Air Canada 747 that had preceded it off the runway at Heathrow at 1:00 P.M. Air Canada would veer toward Toronto over Labrador while Euro-American would begin its gradual descent toward John F. Kennedy on Long Island.

The day was clear and calm. Calm was relative at thirty-seven thousand feet because of the jet stream, but calm nonetheless. The business of transatlantic flight is not complicated and its perils are few. The plane followed the plane in front of it just as the plane behind—was it Air France?—followed the Euro-American bird. Everyone maintained intervals. Everyone watched the routine unfold on the computers.

Three hundred sixty-two minutes into the flight, the plane blew up.

The bomb had been secreted in a case of French bordeaux in the front baggage compartment below the business section and between the two swept wings of the Boeing 747.

The bomb was relatively small. Everything was relative when it exploded. Plastic ceiling panels and floor panels shattered into infinity.

Everyone was dead within seven seconds. There was barely time to scream.

The blip of the plane disappeared from all radar.

The bits of the plane and bits of passengers began a scattered descent over twenty miles of winter ocean. The following plane shuddered as it was buffeted by the waves of explosive air, and a stewardess in first class spilled a glass of champagne on a passenger. No explanation for the turbulence was offered to the passengers by the captain of the following plane, who thought it would merely upset them. They would hear all about it in two hours, after landing at Kennedy.

NINE

T he huge, shabby rail terminal in Naples opened onto the sprawling, shabby, beautiful city that tumbled down the hillside to the sea. The atmosphere was different from Rome. The city was slower, perhaps more passionate, a little sloppy like a businessman whose shirt collar is loosened and whose tie wears a gravy stain. On some narrow streets, the smell of urine on the walks mingled with the faintly garbagelike breeze blowing up from the bay.

Henry McGee sat at a sidewalk table of a trattoria just below the train terminal.

He had taken the express from Rome to Naples and he had been waiting for twenty-five minutes. He appreciated the city sights around him and drank them in with yet another cup of cappuccino. It was the middle of the afternoon and the sun was warm. A sleepy early afternoon. A perfect time to make a deal.

The lead story in that day's *International Herald-Tribune* was about the mid-Atlantic bombing of a Euro-American Airlines flight to New York. Henry had read it twice. It might have been fate, he decided. The target had been picked for him by some minor-league terrorists who wanted to teach the Great Satan America a lesson. As though the bombing of a single airliner would halt the transatlantic trade.

Henry thought it was a waste, an utter waste. Not of lives but of effort. What exactly would the terrorists get? The point of doing anything—especially doing terror—was to get some controlled result. There would be public grief and private sorrow from the bombing; funerals and denunciations by politicians; big lawsuits and a crackdown on airport security procedures . . . and then, nothing. The world would go on pretty much as before. Nothing would have been gotten.

Henry knew what he wanted to get.

At that moment, the fat man sat down in the empty chair on the other side of the table.

Henry looked up from the paper.

The fat man had three chins and a face like a bowl of oatmeal. His frog eyes were large and distended and his fingers were sausage links rolled into doughy palms. He wore a tan suit with a grease spot on the left lapel. His collar wings were bent and his tie was askew. He was perfect for the city he lived in, Henry thought immediately.

"How much money did you bring?" the fat man said without introduction.

"Enough to get you interested."

"Do you have it?"

"Sure."

"That's trusting of you," the fat man said. He had a slight accent that betrayed a Mediterranean—not necessarily Italian—heritage. He tried out a smile that was ominous. "I might have confederates with me. Men who will stop at nothing. They could rob you and kill you—"

The fat man interrupted himself to wave his hands in a fluttery gesture of dismissal. "I suppose you thought of that."

"Cut it out, Juno," Henry McGee said. "I ain't afraid of you or the Confederacy and I get tired of reading the same newspaper over and over just to kill time waiting for you."

Juno stared and blinked. The frog eyes were green and damp.

"You read about the airplane accident?"

"It wasn't no accident," Henry McGee said. "Another pea-brained Middle East terrorist decided to make a statement. No one seems sure of what he was trying to say exactly, but it sure got everyone's attention."

The fat man chuckled. He wiped his hand across his face to remove a sheen of sweat.

The waiter came out from the restaurant with a tray in his hand and waited.

Juno licked his lips and looked at Henry. "Have you eaten?"

"I came to parley, not eat," Henry said.

The fat man stared at the menu board in the restaurant window. "Calamari," he began. "Fettuccine alla mara." He spoke with reverence, as though he were praying.

"Vino?"

"Sì, sì, bianco soave Bolla?"

He paused, looked again at Henry. "Nothing?"

"Nothing," Henry said.

The fat man made a fluttery dismissal with the backs of

his hands. The waiter looked at Henry and shrugged in a very *Napolitano* way and turned to the door.

"You made all the right contacts in the States," the fat man said. He rested his hands on the white tablecloth. "My . . . business partners have vouched for you. You were in prison for two years."

McGee said, "I didn't come here to hear about my life or watch a fat man eat."

Juno's pasty face went a shade whiter. He clenched his fists on the table. "I still don't understand why I have to deal with you to deal with your . . . clients. I'm known."

"Well known in certain parts of the world and not so well known in others," Henry McGee said. "It so happens that you can put your hand on something I want and I can get you payment up front for it. The use we make of it will never be traced back to your . . . supplier, and certainly not to you. Catch on, Juno, or am I going too fast for you?"

"Poison gas is rarely used. It is proscribed in the rules of war."

"There are no rules, least of all in wars. This is proscribed too." Henry pointed to the headline in the *Herald-Tribune*. "Decent society frowns on innocents being blown up. On the other hand, decent society has to have a short memory or else everything would go down the drain. So it invents rules and pretends it lives by them. And it ignores terror, which makes terrorism a bit ridiculous."

"True," Juno said. He inclined his head. "What do you have in mind for . . . the product I might be able to supply?"

"Juno, don't be coy. You supply arms, you supply everything from timing devices to detonators. You are a terrorist merchant and it really doesn't matter a shit what I do with your product once I get it, does it?"

"It matters insofar as it does not trace back to my source or is used against my source or the allies of my source," Juno said.

"You mean you're a square shooter?"

Juno frowned. "I don't understand that term."

"An honest man," Henry translated. He smiled. His smile was very engaging and his even, white teeth were bright in his dark face. "Honey, I'm going to be operating in a part of the world where nobody knows your name and nobody is going to figure out your source. Hell, I know your source in any case."

"You do," Juno said.

"Patras," Henry said.

"I don't know what you're talking about."

"Then I wasted the morning coming down to see you." Henry got up. The fat man waved his hand again. Henry waited, staring down at him.

"Why are you in such a hurry, Mr. McGee. Sit down." Henry took his time.

"Mr. McGee. The weapon we speak of—more properly, the ordnance—is very, very dangerous. Not only in the end result but dangerous to the user."

"I won't shoot my foot off," Henry said.

"What do you know about the . . . material? A point of curiosity."

"Patras has developed Hydra. I know that much. Hydra is nerve gas and untraceable in the body after it does its work because it mimics the glue that connects the central nervous system. I know that much. I talk kind of dumb but if you want me to use the big technical words for what you have, then I can do that too. So stop fucking me around, fat man, comprenez-vous?"

"You are not a civilized man."

Henry didn't even chuckle at that. It was too absurd. He waited. The server came out of the restaurant and put a plate of bread on the table. He looked at Henry as though he might shrug again but decided not to.

When he was gone, the fat man said, "If I choose to deal with you, the deal is fifty thousand dollars per liter."

"The stuff is a liquid?"

"Precisely. It turns to gas when it is heated to seventy-five degrees centigrade. It literally boils into a gas."

"A simple detonator—" Henry began.

"Fawww," Juno said, making a gesture of dismissal. "A cigarette lighter. Well, what do you say, Mr. McGee? Fifty thousand per liter."

"And what does a liter do?"

"You haven't done your homework, not all of it." The fat fingers tore the bread apart and lifted the pieces to the surprisingly small mouth. The fat man chewed as though he had all the time in the world. When he was finished, he spoke again.

"A block of London on a calm day. An auditorium full of school children. No, less than a liter. Perhaps a quarter liter to kill six or seven hundred, depending on the size of the space and the degree of enclosure. What do you want me to say by way of illustration?"

"You said the right things," Henry said.

"Where and when?" The deal done, the voice lost interest in the details.

"Here and now, like I said," Henry said.

"All right."

In the literature of secret dealings, there are always complex arrangements. The simple dealing was much more secret.

So Henry had argued in his first telephone contact with Mr. Juno.

Henry took out an envelope. He put the yellow paper on the table. Juno looked at it for a moment before attacking the wrappings. He opened it and saw what it was full of.

"Thousand-dollar bills are dangerous. I'll have to launder these in Switzerland."

"I didn't have time to buy an attaché case. Fifty of them. Now give me the stuff."

The fat man stared through him for a moment and then looked back at the contents of the envelope. "You have no time for amenities," he said with a trace of sadness.

"Not at the moment."

The fat man nodded and raised his right hand and snapped two of the sausages. The action made a wet sound.

From across the street, a tough-looking Sicilian sauntered to the table and stared at Henry. He carried a paper bag.

"I didn't think of an attaché case either," Mr. Juno explained. "I thought you'd bring one."

"It's in the sack?"

"An old Smirnoff vodka bottle. Perfectly safe as long as you don't drop it on the train," Mr. Juno said. He muttered a laugh this time, as though his heart wasn't in it. The envelope disappeared into his suit-coat pocket. "The key is to keep it cool, avoid direct sunlight, avoid anything that would increase the temperature to seventy-five degrees centigrade."

"Death in a bottle that held American vodka," Henry said. He smiled. "I like that."

"Be very careful," Mr. Juno said.

But Henry was up now, the bottle bag in hand. "I'll be in touch."

"We'll have other dealings?" Mr. Juno said.

"We've only just begun, honey." And Henry was loping up the street, carrying the bottle by the neck of the bag. He had left the newspaper. After all, he had read everything twice about the plane, and he remembered all the names.

TEN

D evereaux floated near the ceiling of the hospital room. He looked down at the man in the bed. It was himself.

The man in the bed had tubes in his nose and his arm. The tubes were connected to many things. There were electrodes attached to his head by wax and more electrodes attached to his chest.

Devereaux smiled down at the man in the bed. He wondered if the man was dying or recovering. He considered the question and saw the irony of it: even if he was recovering, he was dying. Life is just dying. A typically dark thought. Devereaux smiled at his own lack of compassion for the human condition. Yes, that was it exactly. He had no passion, not for life or for death. It made him so detached that he could not speak of it.

The problem, Devereaux decided as he floated slowly

around the darkened room, was that he could not say the things that were in his heart.

He was certain he had been human at one time. He could bleed and even feel loss. He was a man after all but he never considered himself that way. These things were unspoken because he could not reveal one crack in the armor coating of his soul. Why not? Because that single act of weakness would destroy him.

Why did it matter now? He was clearly out of his body, and in a little while, his body would cease and then he would cease. There was nothing beyond the end because the end justified its own means. In this case, life. Devereaux smiled at his jaded cleverness. He could have been a very clever man if he had stayed at Columbia University as a teacher, if he had merely dreamed his Asian dreams instead of realizing them, if he had not become an intelligence officer (as they put it) and gone to war for Lucky Strike. Very clever. All those clever thighs seated in the first row, longish skirts back then at the beginning of the 1960s, but tight enough to reveal all the secret teacherly lusts. Devereaux was prematurely gray and he had compelling gray eyes. How can I get an A, Professor Devereaux? asked the comely thighs. The same way Hester Prynne did, replied the professor. Ah, hell. What were the uses of memory of everything except to burden the soul unto death?

Die and put an end to it, said the floating Devereaux to the man in the bed.

I love you, said the comely thighs. Red hair. Red-haired lover with milky breath and milky breasts and milky thighs, milked hard until his red head poked his redheaded lover, spreading her lap beneath him, feeling all that rage turned into a single tool of lovemaking, enveloped wetly by her purse. Spent himself into her purse. No change? He held out his hand and looked down and saw the woman in the hospital bed, nose and arm penetrated by tubes, eyes closed, breathing, breast heaving softly, unlapped, slapped down, unloved because he had no words and no love, comely, thighs and whispers . . . *Rita*. Rita was dying and he was helpless. He could not save her or himself. This was stupid and intolerable.

Devereaux disappeared.

Devereaux, the man in the bed, opened his eyes and saw palpable half darkness. Felt no pain at all. They had dosed him again and the same goddamned heroin dream had come and he had tripped a thousand levers in memory, remembering words, poems, vignettes of a wasted life.

Goddamnit, Devereaux thought.

"Goddamnit."

He pushed the button beside the bed.

A woman appeared. She stared at him. "What do you want?"

He smiled but she did not see it. He wanted it to do over again. He fixed his mind to make his thoughts words.

"I want to talk to someone about getting out of here."

She smiled insanely. The woman had blood on her lips. She was a vampire and would bite his neck and he would have to sleep in a box with Lon Chaney or Bela Lugosi. He wasn't queer, he wasn't going to get into a box with one of them, he wanted his girl friend and wanted it to do over again, to make love as they made love in the Baie des Anges on the Côte d'Azur that time, lying on the balcony of the hideous Le Corbusier–style building, making love in the Mediterranean sunshine, fondling her bare breasts, her hands pulling him toward her . . . yes, exactly what he wished again: yes.

* * *

The nurse looked up from her *People* magazine and looked at the other one returning from the half-darkened hall that led to the intensive care units.

"What did he want?"

"He said he wanted to talk to someone about getting out of here," the second nurse said. She smiled. "I suppose that's a good sign."

"I'm amazed. He's got enough dope in him to tranquilize a horse."

"Well, maybe he's going to make it."

It was a thing they never talked about, the odds of someone making it. There was too much death to talk about it all the time. You had to make life seem normal and apart from these sick people. The nurse seated at the station desk looked hard at the second one. The second nurse had black hair and pretty doll-like features and too much softness for the job. Her name was Lu Ann Palmer and she was a Baptist. She actually told people she was a Baptist.

The first nurse turned back to her magazine. The story was about the crash of Flight 147 over the North Atlantic last week. A Palestinian terrorist. Well, it happened all the time. What were you going to do about it? Briefly, she remembered her vacation in August in Hawaii. Terrorists were a fact of life but the odds of being blown up on an airplane were still incredible.

She turned the page and settled in. The brief piece was about plans for *Halloween Heaven II* and it passed the time of night, reading about it.

ELEVEN

T he big man had been in the Horseshoe Bar in the venerable Shelbourne Hotel in Dublin for an hour. He had finished two whiskeys and was working on his third. His manner was deliberate and unhurried. He wore a tweed jacket and a white shirt and tie. He had sandy hair and freckles across his wide nose. His eyes were merry and green and he looked like anything in the world except a terrorist. He had been a terrorist for thirty of his forty-five years.

The girl came in as he sipped at the third whiskey. She sat across the glittering bar from him and watched him. When the elderly barman came to her, she asked for beer. He brought her a foaming glass and picked up the five-pound note she had left on the bar.

The room was crowded with the usual lunchtime mix of businessmen and writers, horse breeders and country squires and visiting Englishmen and vague personalities identified with radio or television. It was a glamorous but faded place, like the hotel itself.

He watched her. She wore a simple white blouse and no jewelry. Her face was sharp, her eyes were cynical. Her brown hair was short and swept back from her face.

The big man was surprised it was a girl. They hadn't said it would be a girl. Not that he didn't know girls usually made better terrorists than men, once they were committed to the cause. He thought of Maureen Kilkenny, waiting back at the farm in Clare. She'd terrorize the devil, the big man thought. There was such unreserved wildness in Maureen that he realized the quality was in every woman and he sometimes felt like he was the only man in the world who understood that.

And smiled at the girl across the bar because the girl was watching him.

He picked up his whiskey and carried it around the polished metal bar to her side. He stood next to her for a moment and let her look up at him.

"And who are you?" he said.

"That doesn't matter; you can call me what you want," Marie Dreiser said. "The important thing is you came."

"I came because I am always available to opportunity," Matthew O'Day said. He had a soft Irish voice for a man so large; it was a tenor's voice, and when he was little, he had sung in the parish choir. He didn't sing anymore now and he had not been in a church except to attend the inevitable funerals for thirty years.

"Then sit down and listen," Marie Dreiser said. She wasn't at all nervous. Henry McGee knew she wouldn't have been. They had gone over it, gone over what she would say and what her response would be if the big man said the wrong thing.

"I still want your name," he said.

"Call me what you want. I told you," she said.

"Nobody's that hard," he said. He sat down, the smile still fixed to his broad features.

"Maybe I am," she said.

"All right." Still smiling. "Maybe you are. Let it go for the sake of argument, girl."

"We want a job. It'll involve three people, two men and a woman. Presentable people, not children, not people who can't be trusted."

"What makes you think—"

"Terror," she said. So soft and calm that it amazed him. She turned her eyes on him and he saw that it really didn't matter what he called her, what he thought of her. A moment before, he had felt a vague stirring between his legs. He liked the wild thing you found in nearly all women, the place in them that was too hot and too hard and too wet all at the same time, the thing that was revealed when all the layers of civilization impressed on women were stripped away and they became what they always were. He had seen it in her eyes watching him. But now he saw something else. That wild thing in her was covered with ice a thousand feet thick, and nothing could penetrate it.

"You need money to exist," she said. "For your cause." The last word was very precise; she had put it in italics and surrounded it with quotation marks. "We offer you one hundred thousand English pounds with payment upon completion."

"We're not criminals. What you want is criminals. The

city is full of them. You can hold out your hand and grab a bunch of them.''

She held out her thin hand and draped it on his lapel. Her eyes mocked him in that moment. ''I know what I'm touching,'' she said. ''You're quite right about criminals. We don't have any need for them. We want what you have to offer.'' She let her hand slide up the lapel of his Irish tweed jacket until it rested on his neck.

''I've got a room here,'' he said.

''We know,'' she said.

''Are you interested?''

She smiled then. It was a small smile. ''Perhaps. Later. We've got business, Mr. O'Day. It's better to attend to business.''

''I might want to make it part of the business,'' he said.

''Payment in sex?'' She was smiling and that bothered him. ''All right, why not? Are you any good at it or would I have to pretend that you were?''

''You've got a mouth on you,'' he said. He sat up straight on the bar stool and she still held him by the neck. He might be ten years old and she might be the nun in the parish school, holding him by the neck until he spelled the word correctly.

''Oh yes,'' she said, her voice dropping to a whisper. ''A mouth and a sex. A tongue and teeth and there isn't anything I couldn't do or haven't done, so when I say that, Matthew, I only am being honest. I don't mean to insult you. I can pretend if I have to. I can make you feel like the biggest man in the world. I can do anything, Matthew, I just wanted you to understand that.''

''You're a bloody bitch,'' he said.

They were utterly silent. They were surrounded by sound.

There might have been no one else in the world in that moment.

"Matthew. You have terrorists and we want the use of them. Of their services—"

"We're not terrorists for hire—"

"But you are." The voice was still soft. The conversations in the room formed a roar around them. There had been drinking since eleven in the morning and some of the voices were louder than they should have been. A woman laughed and her voice screeched until it subsided into a giggle. Everyone was damned amusing all of a sudden. "You became that when we contacted you. When you accepted our offer to come to Dublin."

"Who are you?"

"People in business," she said.

"You act like spies, like the goddamned SAS."

"The SAS would not have been subtle. We contacted you through the Czech broker. You know him. We know all about you and your group. About the farm in County Clare and the business you did in Antrim last July. You killed fourteen men in a public house." She smiled. He wanted to pull away from her. "You blew them apart. You and Maureen and what was the boy's name? Was it Brian Parnell? Yes, we know, and if we were SAS, we wouldn't be sitting in the Horseshoe Bar in Dublin talking, would we? SAS would have you in one of their safe houses, wouldn't they? They'd have a noose around your neck and another around your balls, Matthew, and they'd be pulling and tearing just to hear you scream. We aren't hurting you, are we, Matthew?"

Jesus Christ. There was ice and shards of ice were prickling his flesh. He hadn't ever felt this way about a woman.

He pulled back and she let her hand drop onto her lap. She stared at him but didn't speak now.

"I want a hundred thousand pounds. Up front."

"That's impossible."

"Why?"

"We don't have it."

"Then you've wasted my time."

"Sit down," she said.

"I don't think you'd be a very good fuck. I think you just like to fantasize about it," he said.

"Sit down," she said.

"Why?"

"Because I'm being honest. You should appreciate honesty," she said. "We're in the business of terror and so are you."

"Is that right?"

"The Czech connection," she began. She paused and waited for him to sit down. "The arms trade has been interrupted."

"You know everything, do you?"

"The IRA factions have been supplied by Czech armament makers for twenty years. The events—in Prague and elsewhere—have . . . interrupted your supplies, Mr. O'Day. You're becoming terrorists without bombs, without automatic weapons, back to slingshots and street fighting. You don't terrify many people that way. One hundred thousand pounds is a lot of money. On completion of the business."

"Why should I trust you?"

"Why shouldn't you? Would we go through all this ceremony as a joke?" In that moment, the veneer over her English words fell away and she was revealed as a German, as one of the cynical street people of a place like Berlin who think the world is a joke and only the fools don't get it. "We've taken the time to contact you in a way you trust. We've arranged to meet you on neutral ground, in your own capital city. What do you suppose this is about?"

"You still haven't told me why I should trust you. About the money, about anything."

"You have no choice."

"Ach," he said. He started to get up again.

"If you walk away from me, you'll regret it." She shrugged and turned to her glass of beer. "I was told to tell you that. If you started to walk away. I don't know why you'll regret it but I believe it and so should you. I'm only the messenger but I believe everything I tell you. You'll be paid, and paid when the job is finished. I believed it when I was told we need you." She glanced at him. "You should believe everything as well."

"I don't go to church anymore."

"This has nothing to do with church."

"I need payment in advance," Matthew O'Day said.

"Twenty-five," she said.

He shook his head.

"Don't regret it," she said.

"Listen, girlie," he began. He got very close to her face. His fine tenor voice dropped a note and was grouchy around the edges of the words. "It makes no difference to me, girl or boy. If you got to be killed, you're dead. I'm not a sadist, the business has to be done and sometimes it's rougher than I might like it. So don't threaten me about regrets."

"All right." Soft. "This is Tuesday. You'll want to make contact with me Thursday. This place again, it seems a good place for us to meet and not make stupid threats to each other."

"I won't want to contact you ever again, girlie," he said.
She blinked.
He saw the change in her eyes in that moment.
They weren't cynical at all.
He thought they were full of regret.

TWELVE

"R ehabilitation," Hanley said. "Dr. Krueger says it will have to be extensive."

"The operative word is expensive, not extensive," Devereaux said. "I want to get out of here. I don't have access to a telephone, I can't even call Rita—"

"Miss Macklin doesn't know about you," Hanley said. The smell of the hospital room overwhelmed him. It brought back the horrible memories of Saint Catherine's in Maryland where a high-placed Soviet mole in the intelligence service had committed Hanley long before and where he had nearly lost his mind. Devereaux had saved him from that fate. He didn't want to think about it. "Dr. Krueger says it would do her no good in her present state to know that you had been injured. Besides, he advised that your access to a telephone

67

be limited, for fear you would do exactly what you intended, to call Miss Macklin.''

"Dr. Krueger gets around," Devereaux said.

"He's one of the finest neurologists—"

"—money can buy," Devereaux said. "He's a very strange man."

"The explosion that caused you other injuries also caused trauma to your head severe enough to count as a concussion. You suffered brain damage, to what extent it's up to Dr. Krueger to learn," Hanley said. He fell back on the words he uttered with the abandon of a tired man flinging himself on a bed.

Devereaux waited a moment. The silence of the hospital was a palpable buzz. "Do you believe any of that or are you just comforting yourself?"

"We have to face unpleasant facts," Hanley said, turning toward the window. "You've been injured before. That time in Bruges . . . The scars of previous traumas are evident on your body. But what about the scars on your mind?"

"What has that got to do with getting out of here?"

"Dr. Krueger is a fine neurologist, one of the best. We wanted the best," Hanley said.

Devereaux said, "I've concluded a neurologist is roughly a psychologist with a machine to back him up."

"You were . . . damaged. Your brain suffered injuries that cannot be healed. The brain cells do not regenerate."

"Then let's not worry about them," Devereaux said. "I can't recover if they keep me on dope twenty-four hours a day. I don't want any more dope. I'd rather learn to live with the pain."

Hanley said, "I want to assure you that you will be taken care of. That we don't intend—"

"Henry McGee," Devereaux said for the first time.

Hanley blinked.

"Henry McGee," Devereaux said. "He called me in the hotel before he blew up my room. He shot Rita Macklin. I want you to find out about him. Is he still in the country?"

Hanley wiped his hand across his mouth.

"Devereaux. This borders on obsession. Henry McGee is dead or gone. KGB went after him. We gave them all the clues they needed on that matter of the translator."

"It was Henry McGee," Devereaux said. "What does Section want to do about it?"

"Section has no interest in chasing ghosts," Hanley said. "Do you see what I mean? You bring up a dead man's name to explain something that you can't explain otherwise. In all these weeks, you never mentioned that name. Why do it now?"

Devereaux tried a smile. There was absolutely no mirth in it. "Are you saying I'm wrong? I'm one of your agents. I don't guess about things. I thought Section had an unwritten rule about dealing with acts of terror against its own. It kept the balance in the cold war, one side knowing what the other side would do about a wet contract on one of its own."

"Devereaux."

"Of course, perhaps there's no cold war anymore. I haven't read the papers lately."

"The papers assure us we have come through apocalypse unsinged," Hanley said in the same tone of sarcasm. "These are difficult times in intelligence. We have no need for spies when the world is suddenly so open and honest."

"It's the Santa Claus factor," Devereaux said.

Hanley blinked.

"All the adults thought he really didn't exist and now they say they were wrong."

For a moment, they shared the silence like comrades. Hanley was always the control, the puller of strings in Washington, the man who made marks on the map that represented agents and safe houses and operations carried out both legal and black. Devereaux had been code-named November, one of the tacks on the map. And then one day, the world realized the Mercator projection of the earth was distorted and began to question the tacks as well.

"Devereaux. It's time to talk about some things. Unpleasant things."

It was the moment he had avoided for the past three weeks. In the beginning, it was simple. There was a question of whether Devereaux would survive at all. If he had not survived, the problem would not have come up. But now he was hallucinating about KGB agents and he needed reality. Dr. Krueger had been firm about that: Mr. Devereaux needs to be reminded of the reality of things so that he does not escape into his other world, the one that is not real. Dr. Krueger said Devereaux was a difficult patient but that he, Dr. Krueger, understood this because people wanted to deny their incapacities in the area of intellect and memory. He saw it all the time with Alzheimer's patients who wanted to deny that they were suffering from the disease. Did that mean Devereaux had Alzheimer's disease? Hanley had asked. Dr. Krueger had merely smiled a sad professional smile and spread his hands and said, It's only a label, it can't work miracles.

"Devereaux," Hanley began. He looked at his hands. "Devereaux," he began again.

Devereaux waited.

"You recall you attempted to retire from active service six years ago. The matter was aborted. It was a different time then. A different world. You came back inside because there was a wet contract on you and because you needed the . . . security of being part of Section."

Devereaux said nothing. His large hands were spread on the hospital sheet. This was a private room because intelligence demanded it. There was a twenty-four-hour police guard on the door and the policemen had been screened by both the FBI and R Section, though R Section did not, strictly speaking, have the authority to operate in a security field inside the United States. Devereaux even had a private bath, adjacent to the room. He was sealed from the world.

"We think it is time to consider your retirement again. As I said, this is a different time and a different world," Hanley said. He wiped his hands on his trousers and looked down at them as he finished the job.

"Why?"

"You were terribly injured," Hanley said. "Dr. Krueger confirms that you have suffered brain damage that will affect your ability to function effectively in a field environment."

"Dr. Krueger would tell you that cats bark if you asked him," Devereaux said.

"It's quite common for a patient . . . in your circumstances . . . to exhibit hostility toward his physician," Hanley said.

Devereaux let the silence settle between them. He looked at his hands and was surprised to see that he had clenched his right hand into a fist.

"Hanley, I don't really give a damn whether I stay in Section. I want to get out of this place. I want to see Rita and see that she gets well. And then I'm going to kill Henry McGee."

"Devereaux. Your active status has been terminated. In a sense, it was terminated the night you were . . . injured."

"You mean I have no status to perform a sanction?" Devereaux said, and suddenly, grinned. Then the grin faded and Hanley saw there was pain behind the gray eyes, pain in the color of the ashen face. He had lost weight. He looked like what he was, a sick man. The day before, when they came to inject him, he had struck out at the doctor and knocked the needle and syringe to the floor. They had talked about restraining him. They had talked to Hanley about a mental hospital and Hanley had been so shaken that he had actually shouted at Dr. Krueger. There would be no mental hospital, no restraints. Hanley could remember his own restraints, could remember the enforced humiliation that was daily life in the mental hospital he had been sent to. Against his will, as though his will had ceased to matter.

"You have no status. You'll get out of here in time. Rebuild that place you had in Front Royal; I can arrange a transference of assets." Section had bought the place of Devereaux's retreat when the retreat had been penetrated by KGB agents on a wet contract against Devereaux. It all seemed so long ago, the cold war rhetoric, the belief that the enemy was singular and very knowable. Or such was the euphoric mood in current Washington politics that shoved the professionals in intelligence now into dark corners. It was a bitter time for intelligence agencies and Devereaux had to understand that Hanley was trying to get him the best deal he could. A full pension and disability. And he'd even fiddle a way to return that property on the mountain in Virginia back to him. To pretend that there had been nothing in the past to warn against the future.

"All right, Hanley," Devereaux said, and the quiet words

startled him. "I want to get out of here. You know about being locked up in a place like this."

"I was drugged against my will that time," Hanley began. "I . . . was set up; I was set up by a Soviet mole working in National Security. I wasn't really ill."

"Against my will," Devereaux said.

Hanley saw it. What was the difference?

"Get me out of here. You can do it."

"Dr. Krueger."

"Dr. Krueger is to healing what Typhoid Mary was to kitchen sanitation," Devereaux said.

"I can talk to him."

"Goddamnit, Hanley. You owe me this."

And Hanley, unexpectedly, looked at the man on the bed and saw through him as though his eyes had turned to X rays and all emotions and memories were bones, broken and healed, forming the skeleton of the man's life. In that moment, for the first time, he really understood Devereaux, and it shook him because he had no real capacity for understanding others—it was the quality that had made him very good at his job in the espionage bureaucracy all these years.

"I'll do something," Hanley said.

"When?"

"You still have a broken bone."

"It'll be broken in or out of the hospital," Devereaux said.

"Dr. Krueger said your brain wave patterns are interesting."

"So is macrame," Devereaux said. "I want to get out of here. Today."

"I'll talk to Dr. Krueger."

"Tell him."

"He's the doctor."

"You're the payer."

"Your concern for saving Uncle money is sudden and touching," Hanley said. "All right." He nodded, not to the man on the bed but to the man in memory who had taken him out of Saint Catherine's when they were killing him. "All right. I'll tell him."

Devereaux did not speak and, after a moment, Hanley realized he could not stand the silence a moment longer. He rose and went out the door of the private room without saying a word. He nodded to the policeman. He walked down the corridor past the nurse's station, toward the elevators. He took the elevator down to the basement.

Dr. Krueger sat in a windowless office at the end of a corridor. They had arranged this meeting for the time after Hanley confronted Devereaux with his recalcitrance and his violent behavior. Dr. Krueger did not smile at Hanley when Hanley walked into the room. He acted as though it were all Hanley's fault.

"He wants to be released," Hanley said.

"That's impossible. He's on the edge of a breakdown, he is hallucinating—"

"He said he didn't want any more dope. What is it that you give him?"

"A mild sedative—"

"He says he dreams he is out of his body when he has been . . . sedated."

"That's what I mean. The man is going through a very critical time right now. He's hallucinating, he needs—"

"I want you to release him."

Dr. Krueger was a very young man with black hair and a white beard and cool blue eyes. Every time he saw Rita Macklin—and it was every day now—she would either ask why Devereaux did not visit her or where he might be. Devereaux was a very bad influence on Rita Macklin, in terms of her full recovery. Her body was healing nicely and he loved to look at her, at her soft, unlined face and at those beautiful green eyes and to look at the swell of her breasts beneath the soft hospital gown and to think of her in terms of perfect love, to wonder about her.

"I can't release him. It wouldn't be responsible," Dr. Krueger said.

Hanley scowled. "I don't give a damn about that. He's to be released immediately."

"I can't take that responsibility."

"I've taken it."

"You're not qualified."

"Damnit, man. He's to be released."

Krueger stared at him. "If I release him on your authority, I can't have him bothering other patients. You understand what I'm saying? Miss Macklin is not in the government employ. As far as I'm aware. Her eventual recovery is at stake. Your . . . agent . . . or whatever he is, that's your responsibility. But Miss Macklin is my responsibility."

"Dr. Krueger. They were . . . lovers."

"All the more reason. Why was she nearly assassinated in the parking lot of her building? What sort of game is this? I can assure you, the authority of you—of your agency—extends only to your agent. You don't have any right to harm a civilian or put her in harm's way."

"Why would he harm her?"

"She's become . . . very dependent on our therapeutic sessions, our talks, and it's important that the distraction of her trauma, of remembering her trauma, and your . . . agent is part of that memory, not be brought back to her attention.

If I release your . . . agent, and your agent causes harm to Rita, to Miss Macklin, then I hold you responsible. And your agency. I can't tell you what might be the consequences of that. All in all, it would be wiser for your . . . for you and for R Section, whatever R Section is, not to cause further harm to an innocent woman.''

Hanley understood the meaning behind the fog of words. Understood the distaste in Dr. Krueger's voice every time he used the soiled word "agent." There was a threat here and Dr. Krueger could make good on it. What would he use? The newspapers? Television. He would be very good on television, very photogenic with his very black hair and his wispy beard and penetrating eyes. In another time, Hanley might have dismissed him. But Devereaux was yesterday in any case; why not allow the treatment to continue here a little while longer?

Hanley realized he had already abandoned Devereaux. He looked across the desk and saw that the doctor realized it as well.

"Well?"

Hanley said, "No more injections. No more induced hallucinogens or whatever it is that you give him."

"My treatment methods are conservative, are recognized as—"

"No more talk of restraints," Hanley bargained.

"All right," Dr. Krueger conceded.

"He's not an animal," Hanley said.

"No one said he was. He's in a dangerous state. If I had intended him harm, would I be working so hard to save him?"

"So much bad is done for the good of others," Hanley said. He realized it was something that Devereaux might have said. Yes, he had looked right through Devereaux for a moment and seen the frame of the man's life in his bones.

"All right. I won't prescribe further . . . medications. He's in pain but that's his decision. I want to observe his physical progress a few days longer."

Hanley said, "Is this really necessary?"

"For the sake of Miss Macklin," Dr. Krueger said. "I'll release him on . . . Friday. You can tell him that, that I'll release him on Friday if his progress is such that I think it's safe."

"Why couldn't it be now?" Hanley said.

But Dr. Krueger was already thinking he had three days to remove Rita Macklin from her hospital and from the way of potential harm from Devereaux. Three days to secure her in a place of safety where he could minister to her and show her that she could learn to rely upon him.

THIRTEEN

arie made the call from a telephone booth on O'-Connell Street. It was raining and the streets were shrouded in the usual mists made of fog and soot pollution. Dublin was full of din, full of rain and gloom, and she heard all this as the telephone rang and rang. Finally, the connection was made but there was no sound at the other end. She began: "He said he wanted the money right away."

"I figured that."

"I said he would want to meet me in the bar of the hotel on Thursday."

"Good girl. Did he like you?"

"I think he was afraid of me."

Henry chuckled. "He was right about that. I figured on some snag so I'll make this quick. You just stick close to the

Buswell and wait for my call. Tonight. I should be set up by then.''

"What are you going to do?"

"Do you really want to know?"

Marie thought about it. "I'm not afraid of anything."

"I believe that, honey, but there's really nothing to tell you."

She let it go. She hung up and opened the door of the old-fashioned booth and stepped into the rain. The streets were full of people in wet wools hurrying along the walks, splashed by passing cars. Buses roared along narrow ways. The world was close and damp and Marie smiled at it, knowing a secret that no one else knew at that moment in that city.

FOURTEEN

Rita Macklin fitted herself into the soft leather passenger seat. She looked across at Dr. Krueger behind the wheel and smiled. He was a comfort and she so wanted comfort. There was pain but he could ease it for her. Even the other pain of being abandoned by Devereaux. In these weeks, he hadn't called, he hadn't answered her heart.

They were in the countryside. Washington spilled out of its girdle into the suburbs but now the suburban tract town houses were hidden more and more by the ancient southern trees. The sky was very blue and the long, languid autumn of Maryland filled the ravines with colors.

She sighed at the sadness of the colors, the sad scarlets and yellows kept alive by the warmth of the season long past the time they might have properly died. She remembered autumns in Wisconsin when she was a girl and the colors had burst briefly in October, bombarding the hills and forests with explosions of color for only a moment before the sudden death that came in the first snows. Those autumns had been glorious, full of celebration and sacrifice. This Maryland autumn was only elegiac, a sad and lovely poem uttered in a whisper from a pale young woman in a long white gown who lies dying on a chaise propped at a tall window. She sighed again, so overwhelmed by thoughts of death.

She was crying again and he saw this. He accepted her tears. He said nothing and he held her hand when she cried.

She cried so often.

His hand found her hand on her lap. She was thinner now, even though she had never been overweight, but the wounds had drained her. Her cheeks were full of blushes that had the unhealthy hue of the tubercular, though she did not have tuberculosis. She suffered pain but mostly she suffered from melancholy. Why couldn't she end the melancholy?

Devereaux.

She blinked against the tears.

He pulled off the road into a path between the trees that led into a deep forest in a narrow ravine.

"The place is down here," he said to her. But he had stopped the car.

He still held her hand.

His eyes were kind, gentle; they saw through her pain and sadness.

He kissed her.

He had kissed her before, in the hospital. She felt so grateful to him for his patience and kindnesses. She was still weeping while he kissed her and there was something urgent in the way he kissed her that had not been apparent before.

She felt his body strain against her body and she felt her body opening. She was a woman and this is what she was made for, wasn't it?

No.

She turned away from him. He still held her. His face was flushed. She looked out the side window at the trees that pressed all around.

"Don't you want me to kiss you, Rita?"

"Oh. I can't think now."

"Are you in pain?"

"A little."

"I'm sorry if I hurt you."

"You didn't hurt me."

"I'm sorry anyway."

She looked at him. He was a man with a tender heart. If he wanted a kiss from her, what did it matter?

"But will you still come to the sanitarium?"

"Every other day, I'll arrange to be here every other day. I wish I were able to be here every day. They're good people, they'll help you overcome . . . your sadness."

"I think it just overwhelms me."

"Don't worry, Rita. It's something that will pass. We can both overcome it."

"Thank you," she said. And she kissed him. She kissed him the way he had kissed her, the way that would please him. She felt his hands on her body and it reminded her and that caused another fit of melancholy so that she kissed him all the harder to stop the pain or to make the pain worse, she couldn't tell what she wanted. My God, my God. So lost in the world, so pressed in by the colors of sad trees and times past. She was falling through the world and she could never reach the ground because she had so far to fall.

FIFTEEN

T he first was Brian Parnell.

Parnell was from Belfast and was wanted for murder and other acts of terror, including the bombing of a public house the previous summer.

He was sixteen years old and far too young for the job Henry McGee had in mind. Therefore, he wasn't needed.

Henry approached him outside the public house on the Galway road. They had walked to the back where the urinals were in an open courtyard. The sweet smell of urine rendered sour in the ancient slate of the walls made the boy say "phew." He meant it as a pleasantry, a manly bit of male bonding between two gentlemen such as themselves found in the awkward position of relieving themselves at the same time in the same place.

Henry McGee grinned and unzipped his trousers.

Brian did the same and stared at the wall in the accustomed way. Men did not watch each other in such naked moments unless they were intending to send out the wrong signal. Brian was a manly young fellow with a slightly pretty face but he had bucked the mare Maureen Kilkenny more than a few times when Old Man O'Day was away.

"Nice prick," Henry McGee said.

Brian turned; he was so amazed that his mouth hung up and his hand moved to cover his penis.

Henry slashed his throat ear to ear. Blood filled Brian's shirt and mouth. He thought he was shouting though no sound came forth. He stood a moment, feeling the life drain out of him, staring at Henry McGee's dark face and black eyes.

Henry left Brian in the outdoor pisser, crossed into the public house, went out the front, and got into the rental Ford. He had a ways to go.

The second and third were from Kerry and, like typical Kerrymen, they were farmers and simple men of simple wants and pleasures, who had given up the land for a secure job in the Garda. They were assigned to a peaceful district of County Clare out where the *burren* hills fall down to the rocks that edge Galway Bay. They had stopped their black patrol car behind the public house that was on the edge of the bay beneath the hills. They were on duty and it wouldn't do to have a patrol car parked prominently in front of a boozer. Besides, they were drinking milk and just wanted a bit of ham and bread to go with it and break the routine of the day.

They consumed lunch and the next thirty-four minutes of their lives.

The driver was Kevin O'Donnell and he wasn't married

because he was only thirty. Irishmen do not rush into such institutions. His partner was John Rochford, twenty-eight.

That's the way they were listed in the first report in the *Irish Independent*, which bannered the story across the front page.

When Kevin pressed the accelerator, the ignition circuit was completed and the bomb was detonated. The explosive was one pound of Plastique wrapped around the carburetor.

The bomb blew out all the windows of the public house, the front door, the door to the kitchen, broke 312 glasses in the bar as well as the mirror, and made widows of six women in the village whose husbands had the misfortune to be standing at the bar when the blast came. In all there were nineteen killed outright, three who died later at Galway Hospital, and fourteen severely injured, including a nine-year-old boy who was blinded by flying glass. Two dogs were also killed.

By 9:00 P.M. that night, Wednesday night, Irish troops and the Irish Garda had sealed all roads in Galway and Clare counties. It was just as well that Matthew O'Day had stayed in Dublin because he could not have traveled to Dublin from his farm in Clare without being apprehended. The Irish government did not tolerate attacks on itself by the Irish Republican Army and there was no doubt that some lunatic faction of the IRA or of the even more extreme Irish Liberation Army had lost its sense and decided to kill two of the Republic's policemen.

Sweeping, brutal roundups all that day and night resulted in the arrests of ninety-four suspected IRA terrorists across the Republic. And Matthew O'Day spent the next twenty-four hours in his room in the Shelbourne, desperately aware of the hunt going on across Ireland, desperately aware of the simple threat of the girl in the bar: he would regret it.

Maureen Kilkenny called him at midnight. He had been waiting for her call. He was a little drunk and his voice slurred but he thought his senses were alert.

"Jesus, Maureen, I've been waitin' on you."

"Brian was killed. Murdered. Everything's going crazy. Brian was killed in a public house."

"By whom? In that explosion?"

"No. That's the other thing. They came out to the farm and arrested a half dozen of the others. Michael. Deirdre. O'Neill . . ."

She recited their names, and each name hammered Matthew's heart. The best of them.

"Brian was cut. Slashed. The bastard even cut his prick off and shoved it in his mouth. What the hell is going on, Matthew? I'm scared—"

"Where are ya, girl?"

"I saw the arrests from the field. I was down at the ocean with the dogs and I saw the cops coming down the road with their fucking lights on and sirens; when they arrested O'Neill he started to put up a fight and it was what they wanted. The bastards're no better than the Brits. They beat him half to death before they put him in the car. They found the guns, Matthew."

"Jesus, Maureen, Jesus."

"Who the hell killed them? The coppers in that car bomb? Who the hell did this? And Brian—" Her voice caught. She once rolled a bomb in a baby carriage into a Protestant grocery and walked out as cool as anything, right across the street, down to the car, got in the car and they drove off just as it exploded. In a baby carriage. She was talking too fast now.

"Easy, girl," Matthew said, seeing the nameless woman

in his mind. He'd kill her. But then, who was behind her? How many were there? They must have a gang, they blew up a police car in one end of Clare and had time to kill one of his boys at the other end. Matthew's experience told him to be calm now, to think this through. The nameless girl would be killed but in time. Once Matthew could see how many there were. And get some money again. He thought of the loss of the farm and all those weapons, irreplaceable weapons in an arms market suddenly turned upside down. America could supply weapons but that took time and organization to set up. In the meantime, the cells of terror would have to survive on their own. He saw all this in mind while he calmed down Maureen.

"I'm at a public telephone," she said. "It's damned cold but I couldn't make a move until things quieted down. A public telephone someplace in Kerry. I got across on the ferry, I walked for hours, I had some grub in a grocery; then I lit out for the fields. I'm sleeping in the fields."

"Don't go back to the farm," Matthew said.

"What do you take me for? An idiot? Where's this going to end?"

"You gotta get to Dublin. We can get out of here—"

"I'm fucking across the country from Dublin. Am I getting through to you? The roads are covered with coppers and soldiers."

Christ. He had to think. A line of sweat beaded on his forehead.

"Matthew?"

"I'm here, Maureen." He thought about it. "I can't come to get you, that's for sure. There's nothing for it but to hitch or steal a car. Could you steal a car?"

"Thanks, Matthew. I appreciate your help on this."

"Cut it, girl, just cut it. I got me own problems but I'm working on it. Can you get here by tomorrow night?"

"What if I can? You'll still be there?"

He thought about the nameless girl and the appointment on Thursday at lunch in the bar. Yes, he'd still be there. He'd be very careful now and not make quick assumptions because the girl was very dangerous and so were her friends. It was absurd but Matthew faced the fact: the terrorists had been terrorized by the same methods used in the trade. But this wasn't for a cause, this was for money.

Money.

"Jesus," he said, not to Maureen but himself. He began to see exactly what it all meant.

SIXTEEN

Devereaux stepped painfully onto the walk. He had accepted a cane because he needed it. The shoulder was in a flexible, light cast, which meant it was too inflexible and very heavy. His knees were both bandaged. The day was cheerful and warm in the way that Washington can be in November. He realized that he had not really expected ever to leave the hospital. But here he was, an invisible man in an indifferent world full of careening traffic and hurrying pedestrians, broad streets full of trees, embassies hidden by ornate federal facades. He thought it was the tonic he needed most, to be back in the world, however brutal it was.

The taxi took him to the hospital across town. He went into registration and was told Miss Macklin had been discharged two days earlier.

He took another long taxi ride out to Bethesda, staring at

nothing as the car careened up the length of Wisconsin Avenue into the vulgar, expensive heart of the commercial district in Bethesda.

On a premonition, he asked the cab to wait at the apartment building.

He rang the bell a long time and then he rang all the bells in the entrance. A door buzzed open and he went into the inside hallway. Behind a chained door that opened a crack, a woman demanded to know what he wanted.

He told her.

She peered out and saw the cane and saw the way the man leaned on it. A cripple. She had an instinctive feeling of superiority and it supplanted her fear. There was nothing to fear from a cripple.

"She still isn't back from the hospital."

"They said they released her two days ago."

"I'm here all the time." She wore a housedress. She seldom changed her housedress, seldom went out, seldom did anything except watch television endlessly and drink Southern Comfort by the case, which was delivered every two weeks by the liquor store.

"If they released her, she didn't come here," the woman said. She smiled at the cripple. "You meet her in the hospital? You don't look in such good shape yourself."

"No," Devereaux said.

"You wanna come in? You wanna drink? I got some Southern Comfort," she said, thinking about it.

Devereaux said, "I'm sure you do."

She slammed the door as he turned away.

Mac opened the door of his corner office and looked across the newsroom to the reception desk. He had never met this man who had meant so much to Rita Macklin for all these years. He felt a wave of resentment because of the pain Devereaux had caused Rita. Oh, hell. He felt jealous too. He was nearly sixty years old and he felt protective of his reporter, but he also loved her in that part of a man's conscience that can't lie to himself.

Mac crossed the newsroom. It was a magazine newsroom and very modern, full of computer terminals and earnest young men and women in pastel-colored shirts and blouses, men and women alike: cool, dedicated, a bit distant, as silent as the screens they watched their words on, superior to the world around them because they were the Swarthmores and Yales and—by God—Harvards of the earth and they expected an inheritance any day now. Mac was the dinosaur sent among them to remind them of how it was in the old days when reporters wore hats indoors and shouted "Copy!" because words were put on mere paper then. Quaint. They sucked up to him because he still had power, they drank Perriers with him (though he drank martinis), they watched his hands to see if the power would slip at an opportune moment. Mac was old to them and power was in feeble hands.

Mac stood behind Velma at the reception desk.

"She asked about you every day."

Devereaux said nothing. He had not eaten. He felt a peculiar weakness from the mere exertion of riding in taxicabs around a breathlessly alive city he was a stranger to.

"She wanted you and you never came and you could see her sink and sink," Mac accused him.

Velma looked at the curious man with a cane who could cause pain to women. She wondered what it would be like, to be hurt by a man who looked like that. She wondered if she might enjoy it.

Mac said, "Why are you here now?"

"Where's Rita?"

"You could have come to see her."

"I did," Devereaux said. "The night after she was attacked, the same man did it to me. I've been in the hospital. No telephones. No way in and no way out. Security."

"Jesus Christ," Mac said.

Devereaux said, "Tell me."

"Christ, man, you look like you're going to fall down. Come in. Take my office—"

Velma looked at Mac. "Do you want coffee?"

But the men were moving away from the reception desk through the carpeted newsroom, through the pastel-colored blouses and shirts fastened to terminals and keyboards that made *click-click-click* sounds to imitate the typewriter and provide some visceral satisfaction in the silence.

Mac closed the door. Devereaux sat in the chair in front of the desk. There was a view of L Street from the window, which did not commend itself. Mac went to the window and communed with it. He spoke to the glass: "Rita has mental problems."

"There was a neurologist named Krueger . . ."

"Dr. Krueger suggested that she could be helped in a place, a sanitarium that—"

Devereaux said, "Where is she?"

"Dr. Krueger said you might ask, cause her more problems—"

"Look at me."

Mac turned.

Devereaux was on his feet. His face was still ashen but his eyes glittered and there was something in his bearing at that moment that supplanted every weakness that might be in his body.

Mac said, "I didn't know any of this. It was your fault, you and the damned agency or whatever it is that you work for, you abandoned her."

"Yes."

"Then you admit it."

"I hurt her. I thought I should leave her so that she could live normally, that everything I was would cause her grief and death."

"And that's what happened, isn't it?"

"Yes."

"Who shot her?"

"I know. The same man who tried to kill me. I want to make Rita well. Then I'm going to kill him."

"What kind of a world do you live in? Are you insane?"

"No. Neither is Rita. You don't believe she's insane, do you?"

"She's so sad. So broken down. I can't stand to see her fading away, day by day. Jesus Christ, you, people like you, you're really evil, you're rotting meat . . ."

Devereaux said, "Dr. Krueger. He treats her."

"She's grown to depend on him."

"He's a druggist," Devereaux said.

"There's pain, there's sedation, she needs—"

"Tell me where she is."

"No."

"I don't want to hurt her."

"She's going to learn to get along without you."

"No."

Mac smiled. "Oh, the sadist returns. What do you do when you're not pulling the wings off butterflies?"

Devereaux said nothing.

"You gonna threaten me? You ought to know that won't work. I've been threatened. Even beaten up in a stinking Ankara jail. So don't threaten me because I'm not afraid of things."

"Not you," Devereaux said. "She likes you."

"How do you—"

"She told me more than once. She even loves you. You can tell me and save me time. I'm weeks behind the man who did that to her. To me. I'll get him but he's got a lot of time on me. But I won't leave to get him until she's well, if it takes the rest of my life."

"You left her before."

"But that was in my previous life," Devereaux said.

"You've reformed."

"I died," Devereaux said.

Mac watched him.

Devereaux got up from the chair and went to the same window. Both men stared down the narrow length of L Street.

Devereaux said, "I can almost tell you the moment I died. I won't tell her that, it might frighten her. I don't mind telling you. I thought nothing mattered except a few things that I wanted to see and preserve in mind. I had three or four things that I wanted to see endlessly because they filled up everything. I couldn't have those things. Then I met her and she began to show me how important it was, the old feeling I used to have for three or four things."

"What things?"

"It doesn't matter. I can't explain it to you, but you can believe I had those things and they were enough. Then I couldn't have them anymore. And I shut down. Until Rita Macklin reminded me.''

"I don't really understand you.''

"I didn't expect to come back to life a second time. But it happened and now I have to find Rita and tell her whatever words will make her well. She won't be the same but at least she'll understand why she's different now. And then I'm going to kill the man who tried to kill her.''

"Who is he?''

"You don't need to know. He's a terrorist, I suppose. I mean, I assume that's what he does now.''

"This is connected to your agency—''

"I don't work for them anymore.''

"You. And her. You retired once from it—''

"The war wasn't over then.'' Devereaux made a smile that might have meant anything. "Even your magazine says the war is over. Peace and love. The triumph of reason. Men have ceased their quest for domination over other men. Pax Americana, and every day is now officially December twenty-fifth.''

"You don't believe in what you see?''

"I don't care.''

"I want her to be back; I love her,'' Mac said.

"I thought you did,'' Devereaux said. "Let me see her.''

"What if it's the wrong thing? To let you see her?''

"I won't hurt her.''

"You said that before.''

"That was before I died,'' Devereaux said. He turned from the window and looked at the editor. He smiled as if he regretted his words and wanted to apologize for them. There was something in his eyes and in the smile that touched Mac. Something rueful and very honest.

"What are you now? A reborn Christian?"

"No. I'm just alive again but I remember my previous life."

"She can't be hurt—"

"I love her," Devereaux said. In his previous life, he would not have spoken because he thought all words were lies. He was growing used to words. He could reach out into the world and talk. Everything was changed now, he had lost so much, even a fine, simple hatred for Henry McGee. Henry just had to be killed, that was all, it was like killing the bear that time in the woods on the mountain above Front Royal. He wanted the bear to go away but the bear was lazy or crazy or something and the bear became a threat and he had to kill the bear.

"For Christ's sake, what am I supposed to do?"

Devereaux stared at Mac and felt the pain in the words. He waited.

Mac fumbled for a piece of paper on his desk. He held it out.

Devereaux looked at the paper. He handed the paper back to Mac.

"You're going there?"

"Yes."

"Let me go with you," Mac said.

"No. I'm going to take her out of there. I don't really trust Krueger at all."

Mac bit his lip. "I don't like him but I don't much like most medical people."

"He's a druggist. Rita won't get better. Just more addicted. Dependent."

Mac said, "What are you going to do?"

"Where do you live?"

"In town. I live alone in a big house."

"Is it big enough?"

Since Margaret died, he had lived in a town house on Rhode Island Avenue. The daughter was married and had three kids and lived in Santa Barbara. He sometimes flew out to the Coast at Christmas. New York wanted to make sixty-three the mandatory retirement age at the magazine. They might even try to buy him out before then, give him a golden parachute, turn over his office to one of the pastel people sitting out there. When he walked out the door for the last time, he had it all planned: he would go to the lobby bar, drink four giant martinis even though it was the middle of the day, go home to the town house, and blow his brains out with the army Colt .45 he had kept from service days.

He wrote down the address and handed it to Devereaux. As he had done before, Devereaux stared at it, memorized it, and handed the paper back to Mac. "I'll bring her to your house when I get her."

Mac nodded. He felt strangely exhilarated in that moment. She was important and this would be an important thing. Devereaux had already infected him with the life-celebrating sense of doing something important again. There were only a few points left in the world—the grandchildren growing into a strange, tanned breed of Californians, still showing some affection for the funny pale grandfather of the East, but that would pass, one point; point two was Margaret's grave in Larchmont; point three was the magazine; and what the hell was the other point? Maybe a giant double martini in the bar at the Willard. Life was boring. Now it would be important again, for a little time.

Mac said, "You're going to kidnap her."

"Yes."

"And bring her to my house?"

"It's safe. I doubt Dr. Krueger would think you betrayed him. In my experience, he isn't very smart about a lot of things."

"He treated you?"

"He put me on a variation of lysergic acid. I recognized the hallucinations. It was the stuff they tested at Aberdeen Proving Ground in the early sixties, though in a safer dose. I wasn't completely out of my mind, just mildly so. There was heroin as well, I'm pretty sure of that."

"Why are you sure?"

"I was in Asia for five years, Mac."

"Is he doing that to her?"

"Sure," Devereaux said. He said it without any special inflection.

"Krueger will get the police after you."

"Perhaps. Everything can be arranged if you know the people who arrange things."

"So you're still a spook?"

Devereaux smiled. "No. That's what I was. Now I'm something else."

"What? What else have you become?"

"The man who loves Rita Macklin," Devereaux said.

SEVENTEEN

T he nameless girl was waiting for him when he entered the glittering bar.

He sat down next to her and signaled for a Paddy without ice. He watched the girl in profile. A part of him admired her—she was very cool, she betrayed neither eagerness nor nervousness. He could have used a girl like her. Maureen Kilkenny was pretty good, but he wondered if Maureen could have pulled off something like this—to set out to hire a man like himself by using his own weapons against him.

Another part of him was merely waiting for the moment he would put the barrel of a .45 in her mouth and let her taste the metal for a moment before he pulled the trigger and blew off the back of her head. It would come. Matthew O'Day had every certainty of that.

"Well?" she said at last when the barman moved away. She turned to look at him. Her eyes were flat with cunning.

"You and your fellas put me in a bad way. And did you have to kill Brian? There was no point to that, just senseless."

"There's a point to everything," Marie Dreiser said.

"The problem is you've pretty well destroyed my cell, at least for the time being," Matthew O'Day said. "The coppers raided the farm, they got everyone. No tellin' how long they'll be interred. You didn't hafta bring the whole bloody Garda down on us to get our attention."

"They didn't arrest the girl, Maureen. So that's one. And you're two. Now one more man, a younger man. Brian was too young to be useful. Someone with a bit of polish, a bit of manners."

"God, you're a cool bitch," Matthew said.

"Listen, love, this isn't a game. I tried to tell you that Tuesday," Marie said. Her hand grasped the sleeve of his tweed coat. "Everyone assembles Sunday morning in London."

"How did you know Maureen got away?"

"We know a lot of things."

"You're in with the bloody cops."

"Tuesday we were SAS, today we're policemen." She smiled. "You just can't get over the fact that we're very good."

"But who are you? Who the bloody hell are you?"

"Your friends at the moment. Your benefactors. One hundred thousand British pounds."

"Who do we have to kill then?"

She patted his sleeve. "That's better."

Matthew waited.

"You'll find out in London," she said.

"I'm not even sure Maureen'll make it to Dublin—"

"Oh, she will, love. She's a resourceful girl. Like me." Marie rubbed his sleeve. "A girl can get by if she has to. Men just crack up when it gets too hard but women don't break, not very often. We can just bend and bend until men get tired of pushing and then we spring right back in their face."

"You're a fucking feminist."

"Not at all, love. When's Maureen due here?"

"She'll try to get here by nightfall."

Marie grinned at him. She put her hand on his shirt and pushed at his chest. "Would a feminist pay you with sex? Did you still want sex, love? As part of the deal? Sealed with a kiss?"

"You're crazy, you know?"

"Maybe that's right. What do you say, Matthew? Do you want to have sex with me now before your girl gets here? I won't tell her if you won't. Or maybe you'd like to tell her to show what a big man you are and that you weren't scared by the little girl in Dublin at all."

"I wouldn't give you to my dog," Matthew said.

And Marie laughed out loud at that so that several tables of people turned to stare at her. Her face went red with laughter and Matthew only gaped at her.

"It's not your dog I want," Marie finally said.

"That's all you're fit for—"

"You're taking this so personal. I thought you were professional," Marie said. She was still grinning but she took her hand away from his chest. "All right. I won't violate you, love. Maybe you're saving yourself for marriage." She stood up. "Ten A.M. sharp, Twenty-one Dunhill Road."

"You'll have the money?"

"What money, love?"

"Twenty-five thousand up front," he said.

She touched his shoulder and stared into his eyes. She was very close to him. She kissed him suddenly, with something like passion.

He wanted to struggle away from her but could not. She held the back of his head and pressed her lips into his. People stared and the barman frowned. When she was finished, she pulled back. Her grin was insatiable.

"That was Tuesday, love," she growled in a low voice. "Tuesday was different. Now you'll get paid when the job's done. Tuesday I wouldn't go to bed with you but today is different. I told you I'd pay you in sex but you turned me down." She shrugged. "*C'est la vie*, love. London. Ten o'clock Sunday. And I wouldn't want you to regret again, love. Next time might turn out to be serious."

"I'm not afraid of you," he said.

"Next time," she said very softly.

He was angry and it showed in the set of his jaw.

"Next time, you might be on the floor of the urinal," she said.

EIGHTEEN

Dr. Krueger turned on the light in his study and saw Devereaux sitting in the winged leather chair.

"How did you get in here?"

"Sit down," Devereaux said.

"I'm going to call the police."

"Sit down," Devereaux said.

"You can't stop me," Dr. Krueger said. He walked across the room to the telephone on the rosewood desk. The walls were lined with books and paintings. The town house above Rock Creek Park was old and cared for. He picked up the receiver and it took a moment for him to realize there was no dial tone. He put the receiver back on the cradle. Then he saw Devereaux's gun.

"This is crude. What do you want? I knew you were a danger. To yourself and others. I told Mr. Hanley."

"I'm only a danger to you, Dr. Krueger. Sit down."

The thin man went around his desk and sat behind it. He carefully slid open the center drawer. The .32 silver-plated pistol was gone. He glanced up and saw that Devereaux was now pointing the gun at him. It was a very large, dark pistol and Dr. Krueger began to feel afraid for himself. He lived alone. He had treated Miss Macklin honorably, given her comfort and care, tried to ease her pain. He made his silent case to himself.

"What do you want?"

"You know."

"I can't help you."

"Please help me," Devereaux said.

"I can't. You're a sick man and you're in no condition—"

"Pretty please." Devereaux unsnapped the automatic's safety. "Pretty please with sugar on top."

"You're crazy," Dr. Krueger said.

"And you're dead. Do you want to be?"

Quiet.

"What do you want me to do?"

"Write out an order for her release. Now. Into your hands. I'll go with you to the sanitarium. Then you'll drive us back to Washington. Then I'll let you go about your business."

"You're kidnapping her."

"Dr. Krueger. I want you to understand this so that you don't make an eventual miscalculation that might harm you. I want to harm you, every instinct tells me to harm you, but it would be better if I didn't. So you're going to free Miss Macklin and then you're going to forget this whole business."

"You're threatening me."

"No. Not yet."

Devereaux got up from the leather chair. He walked across the room to the rosewood desk. He stood over Dr. Krueger and placed the barrel of the pistol alongside the young man's head, at the part in the long black hair.

He pulled the trigger.

The room exploded for a moment and Krueger made a convulsive move sideways and fell off the chair. The bullet was embedded in the floor. Devereaux bent and picked up the shell casing and put it in his pocket.

"My God, you are insane," Dr. Krueger said.

"Perhaps," Devereaux said. He stared at the man on the floor. "Perhaps it will help you to think so. In any case, that constitutes a threat. Think about it. While we drive out to the sanitarium."

Slowly, Dr. Krueger got up on his knees and then on his feet.

"This is kidnapping," he said again. "You're going to harm that woman."

"Krueger. You're a drug dealer. I know what you are and you know what you are but you've fooled a lot of people. This is a nice house and you make good money. Go about your life. The world is full of people who want your drugs and your soft words. But there are two exceptions I want you to respect: me and Rita Macklin. Stay away from me and stay away from her."

And he fired again, sending the bullet two inches from Krueger's head. It became embedded in a book about phrenology.

Krueger trembled. The tic went from his head to his hands. He jerked his hands convulsively and his right eye began to twitch.

"Do you understand?"

"Yes," Dr. Krueger said. He had to do what the madman said. For now.

"No. I don't think you understand. You'll sign her release and you'll drive us back to the District, but later, after a couple of whiskeys and after I've gone and all you have left is memory, you're going to tell yourself that it wasn't as bad as you thought and you'll call the police and put them on me."

"I won't."

"No. I think I can assure you you won't, but not by anything I've done or said so far."

"Are you going to kill me?"

"Not unless it's absolutely necessary. You'll have to be the judge of that."

"Christ," Krueger said.

Devereaux said nothing for a moment. Then: "We'll take your car. You drive."

"I should call them."

"By all means."

"You've cut the phone."

Devereaux smiled and put the pistol in his pocket. The move gave him pain but he thought the physician could not see it in the half light. "That's in the movies, Doctor. I pulled out the jack. Plug it back in and call the sanitarium and tell them to get her ready."

NINETEEN

T revor Armstrong, president of Euro-American Airlines, carried his briefcase as the entourage floated into the building off Oxford Circus. He thought of the study that showed traffic in London had scarcely advanced its pace in a century, since the horse and carriage. The narrow streets were so clotted with the foul fog of auto and bus fumes that a pall always came over Regent Street in late afternoons. He considered this and a dozen other things because he was a man infinitely interested in the world he moved through.

Strode through.

Dennison was his security man, which meant he carried a pistol. Jameson was his secretary—he didn't trust himself to have intimate business relations with women, he couldn't keep his hands off them—and Dwyer was chauffeur and gofer. His little family. He was so devoted to Jameson that he named his fox terrier after him, a singular honor that Jameson acknowledged with a gift each year on the dog's birthday.

Armstrong was forty-seven, wore a light ginger mustache, and played racquetball four times a week. He wasn't afraid of anything in the world.

There were three elevators in the brass-and-marble lobby of the renovated building and the door was always kept waiting for Armstrong. It was Friday morning, 10:00 A.M.

The elevator brought the silent group to the sixth floor. Here the din of Regent Street and Oxford Circus was muted by foot-thick walls hung with Altman prints, all of them signed artist's proofs. Armstrong loved Altman's colors of parks in Paris and New York, and everyone else was expected to love them too. The colors were sensitive to light. All the lighting on the sixth floor was muted in tribute to the prints. The drawings had been obtained through corporate funds set aside for art acquisitions, and these works were among the things Armstrong intended to take with him when he parachuted goldenly out the hatch just before the big plane of the corporation shattered into a million pieces.

Dwyer veered left at the oak door leading to Armstrong's office and only Jameson and Dennison followed him in. Dwyer was off to fetch coffee for the boss.

Miss Turnbull, the receptionist, smiled in greeting as Armstrong burst through the doors. She was fifty-five, singularly ugly, and the only safe woman in the building. Armstrong smiled at her as she rose behind her desk. And then he saw the man on the plastic chair by the wall.

He only looked at Henry McGee for as long as it took for Miss Turnbull to hand him the morning messages. He noticed a tan, successful-looking man in a seven-hundred-dollar suit of rich blue wool. Henry stared at him.

He swept into his sanctum, Jameson at his side. His routine was set: he saw no one for a half hour in the morning, the better to frame the strategy of the day. The man in the outer office annoyed him. Miss Turnbull followed the boss into the inner sanctum and explained once she had closed the door.

"He said he's from the American FBI," she said. "He said it was a matter of urgency, related to One forty-seven."

No one in the airline spoke of the crash caused by a terrorist bomb. It was merely 147, the number of the flight.

"That's annoying," he said to Miss Turnbull. He turned to Jameson. Actually, he turned on Jameson.

"I thought we had agreement on questions related to One forty-seven. I thought we handled these matters out of office." The statements were accusations. Somehow, this man who had been given the singular honor of having Armstrong's dog named for him had failed.

"We do, sir."

"Obviously, there's a breach. Who's our man at Grosvenor?"

Grosvenor was short for Grosvenor Square, the location of the American embassy that had handled the necessary liaison on the investigation. Police forces of two countries were involved; the terrorist cell had been identified as being based in Libya. Beyond that, Trevor Armstrong had little interest; the matter of 147 was an upset in his plans for "placing" EAA in the middle of the European market in time for 1992 and the restructuring of European trade. Any mishap—any perceived inadequacy in the handling of security at the airline—did threaten in that it caused unwanted publicity, cancellation of expected ticket orders, a general "softening" over a period of a few months of public confidence in EAA. EAA had lost six points in New York and seventy-five pence in London in the exchanges. It was too bad. It would cost the airline settlement money as well. Also too bad. But Trevor Armstrong really wished the FBI and the British police would just go away, do what they had to do, and leave him alone.

There was another reason as well, hidden even from Jameson. EAA was now at a point where its value exceeded its price on the stock exchanges. In fact, broken into pieces around the world, the company would be a golden corpse. Armstrong knew it and he knew that Carl Greengold in New York knew it. Very quietly, both men had been buying up more and more shares of EAA—Armstrong to profit when the takeover came and Greengold to effect a takeover that would dazzle the financial world, spin off into two or three books, be denounced on the floor of the Senate, and generally make Carl Greengold even richer than he already was. Armstrong had met Greengold just once at a charity affair. He longed to be like him.

"Thomas is our man," Jameson said, reaching for the telephone. Armstrong snapped out of his reverie.

"No, that's all right." The boss sighed. It might be better to deal quickly and quietly than to ring up the embassy and get the kowtowers active. What Armstrong needed was peace and quiet and time for EAA to heal from the wounds of the bombing. He didn't want to see the stock of EAA drop further; he didn't want to send the wrong signal to someone like Carl Greengold; he didn't want his own stock holdings to drop—Christ, he was leveraged in up to his nostrils. "Send him in, let's make this quick. We've got Sir Robert at eleven?"

"Ten forty-five, actually." Jameson was Brit; so were Dennison and Turnbull. Dwyer he had brought along from New York because Dwyer was as faithful as an old dog and knew the boss. Funny he had never named a dog after Dwyer.

Miss Turnbull was already gone. Armstrong looked at the messages on his desk. Cargo was the real problem at Heathrow, not only for EAA but the other carriers. Too damned much theft. And then it reached JFK and the real stealing began. The October figures were appalling and he thought Dennison was falling down on the job. He fingered the FBI card in his hand.

"Hello, Mr. Armstrong. Special Agent Cassidy," Henry McGee said.

Armstrong turned up his smile three degrees. Jameson sat at his secretary's desk, pen poised. Henry shook Armstrong's hand and turned to Jameson. "What I got to say is for you, Mr. Armstrong."

"I don't like unrecorded conversation," Armstrong said, moving to his desk.

"You'll like this one."

Armstrong paused. London tried to boom through the foot-thick walls and failed. What was that tone of voice? Armstrong thought about it for a fraction of a second. "All right, Jameson."

The secretary rose, capped his pen, started for the door. Henry blocked his way. Jameson went around him, faintly annoyed by the man.

The door closed.

Utter silence for three seconds.

"Well?"

"Something bad is gonna happen."

What was the accent? Armstrong frowned.

"I don't—"

"Siddown," Henry said, and smiled, his teeth lighting up the darkness of his face.

"Who are you?" Because he knew this man was not an FBI man.

"I know how these things work, Trevor. Public is fickle but has a short memory. Today they remember Flight One forty-seven but, hell, that's water over the dam. If you stopped flying airlines because their security was shit, you'd have to go by boat. Ain't an airline in the world really gives a shit about security except for the Jews and that's because they're playing for real against nations of terrorists. What you want is not to have people think you're just unlucky."

Everything was chill. Armstrong thought of reaching for the intercom, putting Dennison in the room and putting this man out of it. Henry didn't move and neither did Armstrong.

Another three seconds of silence.

"Who are you?"

"What if planes crash and there ain't no bomb?" said Henry McGee. "Could happen. That'd piss everyone off. Like them Caravelle planes in the fifties, kept crashing, people wouldn't take them after a while. Wasn't a bad plane but, what the hell, that's the way it goes. You keep reminding people you run an unlucky airline and they start making jokes about you. Ain't no way to stay in business, not for a middling carrier like yourself."

"You're threatening?"

"Sure. What the hell do you think this is about?"

Armstrong decided. He reached for the intercom at the moment Henry revealed his gun. It was a Walther PPK, a policeman's gun, very neat and dark.

"Who are you?" Armstrong said for the third time. "How'd you get in here?"

"Had a card. Badge. ID. Usual shit. Your security stinks, I think you ought to fire your security man."

Armstrong thought the same thing.

"Here's the drill, Trevor honey. You don't believe me. You gotta have a demonstration. It's gonna come fairly soon. Alert security, all that. It helps to keep the boys on edge. But it don't matter. We're gonna make the first thing small, not involve a lot of people, but it's gonna prove my point."

"Which is?"

"Bombs are stupid. A lot better is something that does the same thing without looking like it's the same thing."

"You won't get out of this building."

"Sure I will."

"What's your name?"

"Felix Frankfurter. What the fuck do you care? The point is, you trade at seventy-seven. You don't want to lose another six points on the New York exchange. You start smelling bad and the confidence is lost. You're putting together a deal, a nice deal, you're going to get out of this airline in a year with a lot of money by selling it to a greenmailer who's gonna break it up in little pieces. And you're gonna sell the airline down the river for a lot of money. I know that. Some of the inside guys know that. That takeover guy, that Carl Greengold, he's gonna tear this airline a new asshole before it's over. But what if EAA has a lot of accidents all of a sudden and suddenly, people find other ways to fly to Europe and the U.S. They ain't gonna buy three-day-old fish. Or an airline that's falling. Maybe Carl would lose interest if the stock started dropping real fast and he'd just back out. How much stock you got, Trevor? I bet you got a lot and I bet you're in hock from tits to ass. Am I right?''

"Who sent you?"

"I sent myself. I even tie my own shoelaces now. Trevor, you got to understand what I'm trying to message. I want five million dollars. You can slush that to me out of your own pocket. I know you can. I know you have to. You're gonna make what? A buck and a half when you sell this company down the toilet to the breakup artists?''

"You don't know anything.''

"Shit, man. I know everything. And you know I know. The point is you don't know exactly what I have in mind."

"You're crazy. I can't be blackmailed."

"Extortion. That's the word you're groping for."

Henry took a step toward him and snapped the safety.

"Look at me, Trevor."

"What do you want me to see?"

Henry smiled. Trevor was frozen dead still. The day had shattered around him. He thought he was embalmed.

"I want you to be afraid," Henry said. "I know you're a little afraid now but I want you to be big afraid. The only thing is gonna make you afraid is losing all that money when you could make a little contribution to the widows' and orphans' fund and be left alone."

"Would I be left alone?"

"Sure. I don't want to play this game more than once."

"Why me?"

"Luck." He smiled. "Was reading about that crash of Flight One forty-seven when I was striking a deal. I figured:

why not you? Did my homework and you were elected prom queen.''

''What are you going to do?''

Henry said, ''I'm going to scare the living shit out of you, Trevor.''

TWENTY

Devereaux had truly frightened Dr. Krueger and he did as he was told for a long time.

Rita Macklin was brought into the small reception foyer of the sanitarium by the director, a man who guided her by the arm as if she might be old or merely crazy. She wore a plain gray dress and a cloth coat and flat shoes. Her hair was loose and wild about her shoulders. She wore no makeup. Her eyes were dull and her hands were small and they had grown old in the past month. She trembled from time to time, as though a passing memory had frightened her.

She stared at Devereaux for a long moment as though he might be someone she had known.

Dr. Krueger glanced at Devereaux in that moment of first meeting. "You see?"

Devereaux saw.

"I am trying to help her," Dr. Krueger said.

"Rita," Devereaux said. He touched her arm. The director of the sanitarium stood behind Krueger, a perpetual smile on his face. He had the sincere manner of an undertaker. He was accustomed to dealing with people in grief.

"Do you see?" Dr. Krueger said, almost in triumph. It was better than he had hoped for.

"Dev," she said. "Where have you been?" She stood apart from him, her green eyes growing sad with tears. "Where have you been? Didn't you hear me calling you?"

"The night after you were shot, I came to see you; I was hit. They kept me in a hospital room without a telephone. They wouldn't let me call you."

"You look different." Sadness turned down her mouth. "You look older. Look at me, Dev. Look at what's happened to me. I was dying and I called you and you never came."

"I'll never leave you."

"Is that true?" And she began to smile. "Until the next time. When you have to leave me. And be about your uncle's business. The next time and the time after that time. I always believe you."

"I never told you before," he said. "I'm telling you now."

"Words lie, you said."

"I love you, Rita," Devereaux said.

She was crying and everyone saw it and no one moved. Tears fell down her pale, drawn cheeks. She resembled a photograph of a refugee, perhaps taken at the time of a recent war, the face hollow and drained and the eyes staring and unbelieving that the body was not yet dead. Numbed by starvation or grief or loss of hope.

Krueger said, "Do you see? She can't be released."

She looked at Krueger and blinked against her tears. She reached for his hand and held it. He patted her shoulder and she went to him and rested her head against him.

Devereaux said, "We're going now."

"I don't think so," Dr. Krueger said. "Do you want to go, Rita?"

Rita Macklin stopped and looked up at the kind face of Dr. Krueger. Did she want to leave? Where was she exactly? Was this still the hospital? She looked at Dr. Krueger's face to see what the answer was. Dr. Krueger shook his head. She saw what the answer was. She looked at Devereaux and saw this different man, a man of ashes, in pain, old around the eyes. Or was she staring at herself in a mirror? What was she exactly? Sometimes she was certain she was someone else.

She said, "I should do what Dr. Krueger wants me to do."

"No. You should not." Very soft, very certain. Yes, she knew that voice. Her eyes opened wide. She saw him. "Devereaux," she said. She had never called him by his first name. She knew him now, it really was him, he had come to her after all these years.

"But what if this is a dream?" she said.

Dr. Krueger said, "You're not dreaming, Rita." Very gently.

"Yes. This is the dream where Devereaux comes, only now you're part of the dream as well," Rita Macklin said. "Is that right?"

"You're confused," Dr. Krueger said.

The sanitarium director finally spoke. "I think she would like to return to her room."

"You're tired," Dr. Krueger said.

"Yes, I must be tired," Rita said. But she stared at Devereaux.

Devereaux said, "I'll never leave you again."

"Is that true?"

"Yes."

"You said words lie."

"Everything is changed."

"Is it changed?"

"Come on, Rita."

"Do I have to go, Dr. Krueger?"

Dr. Krueger shook his head.

Devereaux said, "But you have to go."

Dr. Krueger said, "She's staying here. You've overplayed—"

Devereaux decided.

He took Rita's arm and began to walk her the necessary ten steps to the front doors of the sanitarium. Dr. Krueger said, "You're not going anywhere, I'll call the police."

And Devereaux turned at the door. "Dr. Krueger, come."

Krueger wondered if Devereaux could do anything to him. This was his world. The director was here. There were witnesses.

And the man had a gun and had fired it twice.

"Dr. Krueger," said the director. "Are you all right?"

"No. I'm all right. I'm all right." He took a step toward the door. "I'm all right," he said again. He heard the remembered shot echo in his head and he felt unbalanced for a moment. Terror squeezed him again as it had in his study.

They got into the car, Devereaux and Rita in the backseat.

The director stood on the concrete steps and watched the

Mercedes pull around the gravel drive and head for the road that was beyond the trees.

* * *

They reached Dr. Krueger's house shortly after 8:00 P.M. A soft and warm Washington night surrounded the old houses on the block. Trees filled the sky and the clouds over the city were colored red by the lights from the earth.

They all went inside. Dr. Krueger turned on the lights. They went into the study and he turned to Devereaux.

"What are you going to do now?"

"What's she on?"

"A mild sedative that—"

"Tell me."

Krueger lied.

Devereaux shook his head.

"Look, I did what you asked me to—"

"But you didn't do it well. And you started to lose your terror, back there in the sanitarium. You almost forgot that I could have killed you."

Rita stood next to Devereaux but her hands were at her sides in a completely passive pose. She was hearing the dialogue but it came to her faintly, like the voices on a distant television heard on warm summer nights when all the windows are open.

"You know this is wrong, everything you're doing is wrong, you're harming this woman."

Devereaux said, "Rita. Go outside and wait in the car. It's a warm night."

Rita said, "Are we all going someplace?"

"Yes. We're going someplace."

"Back to the hospital," she said to Dr. Krueger.

But Krueger was staring at Devereaux as though he were

seeing him for the first time. The fear was coming back exactly as it had been before; the moments without terror were illusions, Krueger saw.

Rita walked out of the room, hands at her sides, doing as she was told. She was trembling because the drugs of the afternoon were beginning to lose their hold on her. The bad dreams of night would be coming unless she could get a powerful enough sedative to sleep right through them, no matter how horrible they were. Devereaux was always in the dreams. Sometimes he was watching her and he was smiling because she was in pain. She was bleeding, lying on gravel, crying for him, and he loomed over her and watched her bleed and die.

She opened the door of the Mercedes and slid into the backseat because that was the seat the men had given her when they took her to Dr. Krueger's house. She closed the door. There was perfect silence in the world.

Then she heard the scream.

It was long, awful, like the screams in the sanitarium when one of the women had a nightmare. Or when she had a nightmare and awoke and could hear her own screaming. The scream tore through her thin body and made her tremble all the more.

The scream was a single scream and lasted a very long time.

Oh, God, deliver them from pain and suffering, she thought.

And then she thought of hell.

And then she thought of Devereaux. He would never come to see her again. Even if she was dying.

She was dying, she was sure of it.

Devereaux opened the door on the driver's side and looked at Rita in the backseat. "Come sit in the front," he said.

"I did the wrong thing," she said.

"No. It's all right."

"Where's Dr. Krueger?"

"He said he couldn't come," Devereaux said.

Rita opened her door and changed seats. Devereaux slid behind the wheel and fired the ignition. The car purred into gear and rolled down the quiet block.

Rita stared at nothing.

Devereaux turned to look at her from time to time but they did not speak again all the way into the part of the city where Mac lived.

TWENTY-ONE

Matthew O'Day was having sex with Maureen Kilkenny when the telephone rang in the hotel room.

He withdrew from her body and padded across the carpeting to the receiver inconveniently located on a cheap Formica-topped credenza that was screwed into the wall. The hotel was one of the drearier railroad station hotels down from Paddington Station in a slummy neighborhood of London.

"Yeah?"

"You got five minutes to get to the buffet in Paddington Station. Alone. And that means leave the girl in bed."

The receiver clicked.

"Bloody hell I will," Matthew O'Day said. But he was already slipping into his undershorts.

It was dead Sunday morning, London time. The pubs were closed, the restaurants were closed, the banks were closed, the windows were closed, the traditional English Sunday yawned ahead, or at least until the public houses opened at noon and the alcoholics and the gentry could mingle over bloody Marys and pints of lager. The churches were all open and here and there, some appeared to be filled.

Maureen had red hair of the dark, Irish hue and a freckled, fresh face. Only her eyes were absolutely mad, evidence that she took as much pleasure in murder for the cause as in anything else. Including sex. Particularly sex with Matthew O'Day, who was wham, bam, thank you, ma'am.

Her nipples were erect and she was leaning on her side. "Where the bloody hell are you goin', man?"

Her voice ended in the traditional soft Irish lilt with the upturned note on the last syllable, which is a peculiarity of the Northern Irish.

"A man called this time," he said. "I don't know what's up and I'm gonna find out. He wants me alone."

"Fuck him," she said, making the word sound like "fook."

"I'm gonna fuck them all, darlin', but I got to find out how many there are and what this is all about. So maybe I'll just do as the fella says and you'll do as you're told as well." The words were tenor light and carried the edge of a straight razor for all that.

"You coulda finished what you were doin'," she said, just to say it; she didn't really care.

"Insatiable you are." He grinned.

"No, I'd just like to get meself off once in a while," she said.

"And what's that mean?"

"Whaddaya think it means?"

"Oh, shut your gob, girl, and stay where y'are. I'll be back sooner than you know. We'll find a pub—"

"Fuckin' bloody country," she said. Her sudden hatred of the English overwhelmed her. Perhaps it was sexual tension. "Fuckin' snobs, I'd like to off the lot of them."

"Ah," he said. "Maybe this is about that very thing."

Henry McGee sat on a red plastic chair at a plastic table, drinking lukewarm milky tea from a paper cup that leaked at the seams. The room was bright and dirty. The station was full of echoes and neglect was swept into every littered corner.

"Are you the man?" Matthew O'Day said, looming over him.

"Either me or the fucking towelhead behind the counter," Henry said. "Siddown. Don't order the tea, it's shit."

"Are you the big man?" Matthew said, still not sitting down.

"Siddown," Henry said.

Matthew scraped a chair and filled it. His eyes were nearly as hard as Henry's but he couldn't match the color. Black hard eyes like coal, without any light at all, without any mercy in them.

"What's it about then?" Matthew said.

"The girl got the message garbled," Henry said.

"The bitch in the Shelbourne."

"Exactly. I beat her up a little about it. Nothing permanent. Sometimes she gets to thinking she's running the thing and you have to slap her down."

"So what did she get wrong?"

"About the money. You still get the twenty-five in front," Henry McGee said.

Greed took over. Whatever Matthew had expected, he hadn't expected this. Things never worked out this way.

"When?"

"Tomorrow at noon, as soon as you deliver the package."

"And what sort of package is it?"

"An ordinary package. Federal Express. Except it ain't Federal Express, we're just using their envelope. I made it all out for you."

Henry put the overnight envelope on the table.

Matthew looked at it. "A bomb."

"Not at all. There's a legitimate parcel inside, a book ordered from an American publisher. It's there now and it'll be there later."

"Then what is the book that's worth a twenty-five-thousand-dollar delivery?"

"The less you know, the happier you'll be. Don't forget what happened to Brian Parnell."

"Did you kill him?"

"No. I've got people for that."

"If you got people, I been wondering why you need us then. I couldn't get a third man."

"Matthew. I want to explain something." Henry leaned forward across the table. "I am the baddest motherfucker you ever met. I ain't got time for a lot of romance. I want some things done and I want you and your people to do them. When it's done, you'll be a hundred thousand pounds richer and you can go back to your fucking rathole of a country and spend the rest of your fucking life blowing up British troops and Protestant schoolchildren. I don't really give a rat's ass. Except that if you fail me at any point in the next bunch of operations, if you, in other words, fuck up, I'll skin you alive. That's not just an expression, Matthew. I mean, I actually know how to do it. I'll peel the skin off your body until you're dead. I can make it last a long time.''

Silence. The words sank into both of them.

The early train from Cardiff chugged into the station and doors were flung open and the kind of people who spend Sunday mornings on trains descended to the fourth platform. The train seemed to shudder and sweat, like a farm horse returned to its stall after plowing. Matthew looked out at the platform and saw the words. His life had been hard, spent with hard men—and a few hard women—doing hard things. He believed everything the American had just said. He knew a bluff and he knew a real thing.

"So what about this package?" Matthew said.

Henry blinked as though his own words had caused him to go into a trance. Now he came out of it. The package.

"You deliver it."

Matthew looked at the label. He didn't know the name but he knew enough of London to know the posh address in Mayfair.

"What's in it again you said?"

"A book."

"Bloody unlikely."

"Just do it. Don't pry at the edges of the thing, Matthew. And certainly don't open it if you want to be living tomorrow."

"It is a bomb."

Henry shook his head and grinned. "The trouble with terrorists like you—I'd like to give you some advice—the trouble with you is that you think along old lines. Bombs have been done. Kidnapping's been done. The same dreary people wrapped in towels and mufti, reciting the same dreary demands of the Great Satan or the oligarchic conspiracy.

131

Nobody listens. You terrify no one. To make a pun, it's been done to death, we've seen it all. The nightly news is a bore and we practically expect to see the maps with the X's marked on them to explain this is where Flight One oh-three went down and this is where Flight Sixty-seven went down. Northern Ireland is a joke, man, no one cares but you bloody people and the English soldiers who get paid for it. It's Lebanon but in a different language. You see the Brits moving out of Belfast, Matthew? I'm serious."

"A struggle of four hundred years. It doesn't matter if it takes ten years more."

Henry clucked. He was now enjoying himself. The rotten tea in the rotting cup was forgotten. "You don't get it. You never will. But if you keep your eyes open, you might pick up a few pointers."

Matthew made a face to say he had heard it all before. In fact, it was uncharted territory. A sense of outrage, wounded pride and all the rest of it, had suddenly been replaced by curiosity. It was the cat that had always kept Matthew alive in the dangerous years. What was the Yank's game anyway? He looked at the address again and the name and tried to see it clear.

"And when I deliver it, what then? They'll know my face."

"No one who sees you in that house is ever gonna tell anyone about it."

"Then it's a bomb."

"You've got a one-track mind, my Irish friend. One track. Like that train that came in. You only know where to go because the rails tell you. Go on back to your honeypot, Matthew, and take the package and deliver it after ten A.M. But not after ten-thirty. Then wait in your room for me. And one more thing: send along your girlie to this address at nine tomorrow morning. We'll await developments."

"I don't like to be set up."

"You're not," Henry said. "Trust me. Trust the money I put down. There's seventy-five thousand more coming."

The money had its silent argument. Matthew picked up the cash and the package.

"Ten o'clock," Matthew said.

"Now you got it," Henry said. In fact, Matthew didn't know what he had taken with that package. Not at all. The thought made Henry grin again.

TWENTY-TWO

$\mathbf{M}$aureen was dressed for action: tight jeans, black sweater, black beret, black raincoat. Seeing her with her long, reddish hair and gray, unfeeling eyes, you could imagine the face of the assassin or the terrorist. She might as well have an Uzi under that long coat, might as well be waiting to blow up a school bus, or just waiting for death to deal or be dealt.

It was exactly nine o'clock Monday morning, twenty-three hours after Matthew took the package from the man in the buffet.

Matthew had explained about the man he met in Paddington Station and the package and the mission, and when Maureen had complained she didn't understand any of it, Matthew had grown angry because he was confused as well. The words that denigrated the struggle—the mocking, cynical words of the stranger in the buffet—had wounded him more than he knew. He told her to shut up and even slapped her, but that had not cowed Maureen. She had come back at him, teeth and hands and rage, and the tussle had alarmed the manager of the hotel, a small-boned Indian man who smelled of curry and had brown teeth. He threatened to call the police and that had calmed them down—not ended the fight, just made it a matter of silences and glowering looks at each other. Maureen had spent the afternoon by herself, walking the streets of the great, gray city, thinking about things, thinking about Matthew, thinking about poor bloody Brian lying in his own blood in the urinal of that public house. Most of all, thinking about the package and the man in the buffet who had so threatened Matthew and who had probably caused all the troubles that had fallen on the group in the last several days.

Maureen was certain she was going to meet him at this address.

It was an attached town house, graystone and Georgian, part of a street full of similar houses in a treeless neighborhood near Hyde Park. Heavy traffic noises from Maida Vale echoed down the block and made the curious, peopleless silence of the houses that much more sinister. There'd never be children on this block, Maureen thought; it was barren from birth.

She rang the bell.

Henry McGee opened the door for her. He was dressed as she was, ready for action. He wore a black pullover and black fatigue jacket.

"Right on time, honey," Henry said. "Is your boyfriend following the plan?"

"He runs our operation," she said, explaining. She looked at him closely. He was probably as old as Matthew but there was a difference. The eyes weren't cold. Matthew had cold eyes, even in the middle of operations. This one was just as hard in the eyes but there was something else. Something that burned.

"Anything you say," Henry said, smiling. He led her to the right, to an old-fashioned parlor filled with embroidered things and wallpaper flowers. The lamps had fringes on the shades. The room made her smile because it was bizarre in this context. Henry saw the smile. He decided something.

"I'm just borrowing it for the time being," Henry said.

Maureen looked around the room. She might have been a child in her aunt's house in Dublin. Framed photographs sat on a sideboard, and above the fireplace was a photograph of Queen Elizabeth II as a young woman. Her aunt had a photo of the Pope.

"You have quaint friends. English friends." She turned and gave back his blazing look.

For a moment they stood apart and then Henry smiled again. "You take your friends where you can get them," Henry said. "You strike me as not being as dumb as Matthew. I'm not saying you're smart but you can show me that later."

"I've got nothin' to prove to you. I don't even know why I'm here."

"Because I wanted you here."

"And you've not the control of me—"

"Save it," Henry said. It was like a snap—quick, savage, the sense of necks breaking.

"What the bloody hell is this about? And why'd you kill Brian Parnell?"

"Brian Parnell wasn't important. It was the message that was important and Brian didn't figure. You figure—"

"And if I'd been caught in the roundup?"

"But you weren't, girl. You weren't. I want you to sid-down and shut up and listen a bit."

"I'll stand."

He chuckled and shook his head. "Then stand." Henry sat down on a stiff Chippendale. He crossed his legs. He looked at her for a moment.

"One million pounds. English pounds. That's one million six hundred thousand dollars by the morning paper, and I like to think in terms of dollars because it makes the money more real."

"What money?"

"I told Matthew it was a hundred thousand pounds to him. Well, it's nine hundred thousand to me. What I need here is someone I can trust and that's going to be you."

"To do what? Rob a bank?"

"I can take care of that, honey. Robbin' banks is easy but banks just don't have that kind of cash lying around. Better that you rob the people who put their money in the banks. Let them make the withdrawals. On your behalf. You and me, girl, are in partnership, and there's only gonna be two partners in the long run. What we need is a setup. It's gonna be you or it's gonna be Matthew. Which do you want it to be?"

"You're crazy. I'll not betray—"

Henry McGee held up his hand. "Betray. What do you think this is about? Matthew is greedy and just a little bit too stupid but I'm surprised you haven't noticed that before. Matthew's got you believing in him and that makes me wonder about you. You want betrayal as a reason for something, then you ought to look at Matthew O'Day, the famous Irish patriot and terrorist, who sold out his kith and kin for a lot less than thirty pieces of silver.''

She felt a sense of disorientation. She would sit down after all. The room was too familiar, too old, too much a part of her past; yet she had never been in this room before.

''Matthew is getting out of the game. Too long in the tooth—''

''Who are you?''

''You might say I was with SAS. Or something like that. On the other hand, I'm probably not.''

Jesus Christ. Maureen felt all the blood drain from her face. She stared at the hard man across from her but he was still smiling and he hadn't moved. She looked at the window, the doorway.

''Don't,'' Henry said.

''What the hell game is this then?''

''A little game of getting rich. Y'see, you asked me about Brian. Well, I got Brian from Matthew. He said Brian was humping you and he was willing to betray him for a consideration. The consideration was that we wouldn't kill him. We thought about it and took him up on it—''

''You killed those people in the pub on Galway Bay—''

''Not at all. Do you think we'd kill innocent people?''

''You do it all the time—''

Henry smiled. ''Was he? I mean, Brian. Was he humping you like Matthew said?''

For the first time since coming into the strange room, she felt fear. It was hard to put her finger on it but there was a certain madness to this man, a madness without edges or depth. Not hatred, just cruelty for its own sake. She looked at the door again.

"I don't believe you. I don't believe Matthew O'Day would betray any of us—"

"And the farm. Who knew about the farm except Matthew? And the cell? And who turned the lot of you in to the Garda after the bomb went off in that public house and killed all of those poor people?"

"You killed them yourself."

"If you want to believe that, fine."

Silence.

A clock struck the quarter hour with the first notes of Westminster chimes. The room was chill and the silence penetrated her bones until she shivered.

"Maureen, everything in this world is about money. Your cause, your terrorism, your puny strikes against the queen by blowing up postmen in Belfast . . . It's pathetic when you come down to it, because nothing matters except the money. If your bunch had expended all its energies in getting money the last twenty years, you could have bought Ulster from the English, you could have made every Catholic family in Derry a millionaire. Christ, you're all a lot of losers. I almost regret wasting my breath explaining this to you."

"You're a Yank, you're not SAS. What the hell do you have to do with us?"

"Honey, my nationality is green, the color of money. So Matthew came to Dublin when we asked him and he got the proposition presented to him and he took it."

"He did not."

"He told me about Brian and said he mostly wanted to get Brian. So we took care of that for him."

She stared.

"Why do you suppose he was in Dublin those three days when all hell was breaking loose in the west of Ireland? He's no fool. He sold you, all of you, including little Brian of the big dick.''

"You bastard," she said.

"One of my associates did the deed for Matthew, to show our good faith. Cut his throat and cut off his dick. What do you miss most, Maureen? His life or his prick?''

She crossed the room like a cat and struck him. She was very strong and the blow told. Yet he shook his head and stood and faced her. She struck him again. He smiled. She struck him a third time and then he hit her very hard and the pain went all through her belly and into her chest and she couldn't breathe and she was going to die. She fell to the floor to make it easier to die. She waited for death and yet involuntarily struggled against death and was surprised that the struggle seemed to have meaning. She did not die. Breath came. The pain remained but she could breathe. She blinked her cold eyes and saw Henry standing over her.

"Christ," she said. She heaved another cubic foot of breath into her lungs. "Christ," she said again.

She struggled to rise.

Henry sat down again.

She stood up uncertainly, feeling the pain in the center of her body, staggered to the horsehair couch, and sat down. She rubbed her belly.

"I was saying," Henry said. "I need a fall guy. Matthew picked you. I pick Matthew."

"A fall guy?"

"An American expression, honey, I'm sure you've seen it in the movies. It means the mark, the setup, the guy who gets dumped on while the other guys get away."

She waited, letting the breath sob into her.

"Matthew is delivering a package this morning. You know

that. The guy he's delivering it to is an American businessman living in London.''

"It's a bomb."

"I told you. It's a book. It's a novel called *Halloween Witches*. It's supposed to be a fairly lousy book, I don't know, I don't read novels. The point is, the writer lucked out and the book became a movie. You wanna know what the movie is?''

She didn't speak, didn't move. The pain was going down but it was still there, glittering inside her like the eyes of this man.

"*Halloween Heaven*."

Maureen stared.

"They were showing that movie on Flight One forty-seven when the Arabs blew up the plane. You know. The plane that crashed a few weeks ago."

"I don't get it."

"The man runs the fucking airline. His name is Trevor Armstrong, sounds like a fuckin' Brit but he's a New Yawk boy, Groton and Harvard, doncha know. We're sending him a copy of the book. That's the message. The important thing right now is the messenger. Matthew is doing this because of his expertise in bombs. He's confused but he thinks it might be a bomb. He's working for me, for us. He sold you all when he blew up that police car outside the pub on Galway Bay. He got fifty thousand dollars for that one. I'm sure he never told you that. And we also gave him Brian Parnell's dick. Don't you get it? He wanted that, he wanted us to mutilate him. Bloody, isn't he? But you know that, Maureen, you worked with him.''

Silence. She thought about it. She stared at the hard man

and the silence ticked along. When she spoke, her voice was cold and low and the brogue was broader than it had been.

"And what's this about then?"

"Aren't you paying attention? What the fuck do we want with the IRA except terror? We're hardly hiring you for your expertise in folk singing. About terror, honey. We're going to wring a little money out of an American businessman who can't afford to have another one of his airplanes blown up. Not right before Christmas and not with that other plane still in everyone's mind."

"Are you gonna blow up a plane then?"

Henry smiled. It was a dreamy smile, as though he saw something that no one else in the world could see.

"Not at all, honey. I'm not a terrorist. I don't have any cause. I just need a fall guy and a little time and a little luck."

"That bastard," Maureen said finally, beginning to see it, beginning to see the betrayal that Matthew was capable of, beginning to see why Brian's body had been mutilated, beginning to see everything that Henry McGee had been trying to get her to see. "That bastard," she said again.

And Henry saw that he had her.

TWENTY-THREE

M atthew O'Day delivered the envelope at 10:23 A.M. The housekeeper took it and signed for it.

The entire transaction took ten seconds and in that time, Marie Dreiser managed to click off nineteen frames. She used a Minolta A2 autofocus with machine drive and ASA 400 black-and-white Kodak film. The camera was practically foolproof, which was just as well because Marie had never used one before in her life.

She stood at a new-style phone booth wearing a tan raincoat and black jumpsuit. Matthew O'Day never saw her. His eye was on the housekeeper and the package, which he was still certain was a bomb.

He hurried down the street away from Marie and toward an enclosed park. She finished the roll of film by clicking shots of his retreat. When the roll was finished, the camera rewound the film automatically. She popped the back, took out the film, and slipped it into her pocket.

The whole thing was exciting; it made her blood run faster. She felt very alive. It was too bad about the one killing but Parnell was a terrorist and Henry said she shouldn't feel sympathy for terrorists.

When the news had flashed on the television set in the Buswell Hotel in Dublin about the explosion outside the public house, she had thought of Henry and she had thought of running away. There was murder—didn't she want to kill the old priest in Rome who had a hand in the death of her Michael?—but this was slaughter, this was beyond revenge or even anger.

She had waited to see the truth of the thing in Henry McGee. He had come back to her at midnight, his clothes dirty, his face wild. She had accused him of the bombing and he had smiled at that. He said the bombing was "just serendipity," just a coincidence.

Henry had not blown up the people in the public house. Henry had told her that. "I can't be in two fucking places at the same time," he had said to her when she had asked him. "But I'm fucking going to use it. Let 'em think we're omnipotent. That's the point. Let em think we got a gang here instead of just a crazy German girl and one old man."

He wasn't an innocent and she didn't have to worry about him as she had worried about the one innocent she had ever met in her life. Michael. She still thought of him. She had tried to save him and she could not and then Henry had come along and he was good enough, he was warmth in winter in bed, he was pleasure; and if he caused her pain at times, well, what of it? Her life was pain, and pain was existence, wasn't it? People got their pleasure through the pain of others. When she stole sausages from the delicatessen, the old man in the straw hat behind the counter knew, he knew her pain; he had put his hand under her skirt for a long time, he had molested her—how many times was it?—just touching her and exciting himself in the process and putting his fingers all over her. Was she going to feel ashamed of herself because of what he did? Hell no, they could all go straight to hell if they thought she was going to be ashamed or was going to be afraid of them because of what they could do to her. She'd do it to them first.

So Henry had only killed a terrorist named Brian Parnell, and around the same time, some other mad group had blown a police car to smithereens. What did it matter to her? Henry was there and still full of warmth and life and she had lived too long as a little rat girl alone in the depths of Berlin and she needed him because she needed warmth. She had accepted Henry's lie about the public house bombing because she needed to believe in someone, not to end the pain of existence but to make it endurable.

Michael.

When she thought of Michael, a whole universe of déjà vu came upon her to disorient her to the world around her. Thoughts of her lamb, of poor dead Michael triggered thoughts of the night they had made love in a cheap Paris hotel, which triggered the thoughts of his death on the Tiber River bridge in Rome, which triggered so many things. She suddenly remembered Devereaux, who had saved her life. Devereaux had no gentleness either, he was as hard as Henry McGee except there was a quality of pity in him that mitigated all the hardness. He knew what life was, just as Marie did, they saw it in each other and they saw the quality of pity in each other too. Life was agony, just one long scream from the moment of birth to the final silence.

She realized she was crying.

She usually didn't cry but sometimes there was a mixture of things, thoughts of Michael, thoughts of what could have been—oh the hell with it, it could never have been like that for her because she was nothing, just a dirty little survivor of the streets of her mother, Berlin, just a girl to be used and to use, just a slut and a whore and feel me up, mister?

Henry had explained it carefully. They were going to steal five million dollars from the man who ran the airline. Trevor Armstrong. They were going to terrorize him first. Part of the terrorism was using this Matthew O'Day to deliver an innocent package to the house and then sending photographs of Matthew O'Day to the SAS. A known IRA terrorist like Matthew O'Day was in London, delivering packages to a respected American businessman named Trevor Armstrong, president and chief operating officer of Euro-American Airlines, which now traded at seventy-six and was on the verge of being leveraged into a takeover by a group led by Carl Greengold. The IRA was going to threaten to blow up Euro-American Airlines. The way it would work, Henry explained to her, was that British intelligence, in the form of the dreaded SAS, would authenticate the threat and where it came from. Only Henry would know the truth, and Trevor Armstrong, who would agree to the blackmail. Marie didn't understand all of it but she had nodded agreement to Henry that night in the Buswell Hotel in Dublin.

Henry was clever and he wasn't too concerned with rough edges. That suited Marie. She had never become accustomed to gentleness so she didn't know what it was.

That was a lie. Yes she did. She had known one lamb in the world and he was dead because the world was too hard for innocence to survive.

Damn her tears. She wiped at her eyes roughly with her hand and her eyes hurt her. Everything she knew was hurt and pain. Why shouldn't she be rich with Henry? Damn the world and tears.

The photo shop was on the Edgeware Road and it was one of those places where the photographs could be had in less than a day. She told the boy behind the counter what she wanted. Henry had explained it: one set of prints as soon as possible. It was all part of his plan and he never explained all the parts of it. Henry said she didn't need to know everything, it was just important that she trusted him and did what he told her to do.

No. Henry didn't blow up that police car outside that pub in Ireland and he didn't have the blood of all those dead people on his hands. Yes, he'd killed a few people in the service of his country—depending on which country it was —but he didn't take any pleasure in it and he had only killed Brian Parnell who was nothing but a fucking terrorist anyway. Oh, yes. She believed him and held him and let him plunge into her lap with his body and impale her with his lovemaking and, yes, she believed him as she closed her eyes and felt him in her and, yes, she had to believe him and hold him and feel his warmth, even if it was roughly given and full of deceit and lies. Yes, yes, yes.

"And how many prints, miss?"

She thought about it.

"Two," she said in her accented English. "Two sets of prints will be fine."

TWENTY-FOUR

H enry McGee broke into the cellar of the house in Mayfair at 11:31 A.M. He placed the small vial on the wooden workbench and dropped in two large tablets. The chemical reaction began immediately. The liquid was turning to gas.

He wore a gas mask.

The gas rose quickly and was at the level of the floorboards of the first floor when Henry made it out of the cellar through the back door. He rushed along the path that led to the alley behind the buildings. There were brick walls between the individual plots of backyards and all the properties had high wooden gates on the alley, to provide privacy and security.

The housekeeper saw him from the kitchen window and thought to call the police.

It was the last thought of her life.

There were three other servants in the house on that final morning of their lives.

TWENTY-FIVE

H anley did not drive and did not have a chauffeured automobile. It was a perk of office he deserved as Director of Operations for R Section but he had a curious, populist distaste for the idea of public servants riding in limousines. He was from Nebraska and entering his final years of government service. He had been with R Section since the beginning and had climbed slowly and more or less honestly through the ranks. He had never been "in the field" and had an odd sense of having lost something because of that lack. He had never married; his relatives were all dead; he had his job in R Section and his friendship with the director of R Section, Lydia Neumann; and he had some men he could relate to and even have lunch with at times. He never took a vacation because there was no place to go and a vacation would merely have meant separation from his real life.

No. He was not a friend of the former agent, Devereaux, known in files as November. No, not at all.

The taxi swept through the rain down Pennsylvania Avenue toward the Capitol. Thunder clapped across the boulevards of the city and filled the circle parks where the dope dealers and homeless mingled under the Southern trees. Hanley studied the beaded seat of the driver.

"What is that thing you're sitting on?" he said.

"Beads, man. Help you stay cool in summer. Help your back. Sit on beads good for you when you driving."

"They don't look comfortable."

"They are," the driver said, challenging him in the rear-view mirror.

Hanley sighed. He settled back into the discomfort of the dirty vinyl interior. Everything about the day was full of discomfort. Irritation. Damn Devereaux. The man was bound to cause this trouble and Hanley should have seen it coming.

The taxi swept into the square before the Capitol and skid-ded to a stop in front of the Irish saloon. An Irish saloon, Hanley thought: how appropriate.

Twenty-seven hours before, all hell had broken loose. And it was still loose in the streets. It was all Devereaux's fault.

Hanley paid and demanded a receipt. He kept his accounts regular; he was probably the most honest employee in the United States government, including the president.

He crossed the sidewalk and pushed into the saloon. It was 11:30 in the morning and only a few drinkers had slipped away from their offices to begin another day with the bottle.

Devereaux stood at the bar. A glass of beer sat on a card-board coaster in front of him. Hanley came up.

"I don't know why I'm here."

Devereaux looked at him. There was no mercy today for

anyone. "Because you have to be here. Because you need me."

"You kidnapped Miss Macklin."

"Yes."

"That's a criminal act, even for an intelligence officer who has involved himself in criminal acts before and been exonerated by his long-suffering government."

"Drug dealing is also a crime. The jails and the parks are full of dealers."

"Dr. Krueger was found in his study. He was hallucinating. He is now in Saint Elizabeth's Hospital, in the psychiatric ward. They say he took LSD, they don't say how much, they don't even know if his sanity will return. He stabbed himself, they said, he stabbed himself in the palm of his left hand with some kind of spike, the sort they use in offices. The police found that in his study as well."

"Those who live by the sword," Devereaux said.

"You've become a philosopher. The director of the sanitarium where you . . . abducted Miss Macklin . . . he identified you."

"And Dr. Krueger. We did it together."

"And Dr. Krueger then decides to OD on LSD."

"Did they find drugs in his house?"

"A lot of them. A cornucopia of pharmaceuticals. But he is a doctor."

"He's a drugstore with two feet," Devereaux said.

"God, you are a bastard, a murderous bastard," Hanley said. "It's good we've separated you from Section. You've gone too far."

"Too many times."

There was frustration in Hanley's voice and in the tremble of his hand.

The barman came up.

Hanley said, "Beefeater martini, straight up. With an olive," he said.

The barman turned away.

"It's not even noon yet," Devereaux said.

"You've interrupted my lunch hour."

"No. It's your turn."

"We've cleaned up the mess you've made. You knew we would."

"Yes."

"We can't be caught in a scandal. You're blackmailing Section."

"My loyalty is unquestioned," Devereaux said.

Hanley frowned at the sarcasm.

The martini came and Hanley sipped it. It wasn't the same as the martini he had every day at lunch in his usual place where they always made him a well-done cheeseburger with onion and a martini and a little kosher dill on the side. He had taken to onions in recent years. Hanley loved his routine and felt lost without it today.

"Where is Miss Macklin?"

"Safe."

"But where?"

Devereaux stared at him. "It's none of your business. Your business is giving me a trail to Henry McGee."

"I told you yesterday that he didn't exist."

"That was yesterday."

That was the morning when the police found the raving Dr. Krueger in the study of his home. That was the morning of inquiries from police about a former patient of Dr. Krueger's named Devereaux who had been released the day before from hospital and who had appeared with Dr. Krueger at a private sanitarium about 8:00 P.M. the previous evening and secured the release of another of Dr. Krueger's patients. The police wanted to question someone in authority inside R Section and Hanley had pulled strings and blown whistles until the lower-level cops were squelched by the higher levels. There would be no inquiry; there would be no pursuit at any level. Until and unless Dr. Krueger recovered his senses and could tell coherently and believably how it was that he ingested a controlled substance at home and why his house was full of other controlled substances, including cocaine, heroin, marijuana, and even a small quantity of crack.

"I made a scan," Hanley said.

"I don't understand the term."

"We're in the computer age. There is too much information. It floats around the world like a cloud. A scan is the act of penetrating the cloud for a specific raindrop."

"You've become poetic in your declining years."

"The Irish special branch made known to the SAS in Britain the description of a suspected terrorist who killed another suspected terrorist in a public house in the west of Ireland. It was a ghastly crime in its details, involving sexual mutilation."

"Why did it become a matter big enough to circulate to England?"

"Because of what happened two hours after this murder. Two hours later, a public house was damaged when a police car parked outside it was bombed. In the Republic of Ireland, not the north. Two policemen were killed and a number of people in the public house. Yes, the inevitable eyewitnesses said they saw a man who had visited the public house earlier.

An American, they thought. They described him. Guess who he looks like? The man who had killed the terrorist earlier. And guess who they both looked like?''

"Henry McGee."

"They don't have a name because they don't know he exists. They think he might be Irish or English. Being an American doesn't seem to fit for them; apparently, Americans are supposed to be the victims of terrorism, never the perpetrators. But they routinely put the description on the scan for American eyes. I picked the description out of the scan. We should inform them."

"We should not."

Hanley stared at Devereaux for a moment. Then he looked around the large, dark room. ERIN GO BRAGH, said one sign on a wall, left from Saint Patrick's Day. ENGLISH OUT said another, more heartfelt, scrawled on plaster. It was a dreadful saloon.

"Why did you choose this place to meet?"

"It has a front door and a back door. In case you weren't friendly and had second thoughts. Besides, I like the beer."

"You have caused me great professional discomfort. These are trying times for Section. Budgets are to be cut; manpower is to be cut. The world of espionage and intelligence is under siege because the world has become a nicer place."

"So it seems. All those smile buttons in the seventies finally had some effect. Like prayers for the conversion of Russia that Catholic schoolchildren recited after Sunday mass in the fifties."

Hanley didn't know what to say. He looked at his drink. He looked at the wall filled with whiskey-company mirrors.

"So Henry McGee exists," Hanley said. "More important, he seems to be involved in terror."

"He has always been involved in terror. I tried to tell you that from the beginning. And he worked for R Section once and it would be a terrible embarrassment to Section to have a terrorist traced back to it. Especially at a time of budget cutbacks and such."

"You are being sarcastic," Hanley said.

Devereaux smiled. It unnerved the other man.

Hanley said, "We bit the bullet on that long ago. We went after him when he defected to the Soviets. We took our heat and we put him in prison. But he escaped and—"

"Yes. That's the big 'and,' isn't it? He collaborated with us again. That's the part Section can't allow to get out. And it might get out as long as Henry McGee is alive and there's a chance that someone might catch him. The Irish. Or the Brits. If SAS used some of their preferred methods of torture, they might accidentally trip across information they didn't know Henry had. And where would that put you, Hanley?"

Why was this man shoving him into a corner? Hanley looked around wildly for a moment, as though he contemplated physical escape. But the doors were all there for the opening and closing. He could leave any time he wanted.

"You said he existed. You said he tried to kill you and Miss Macklin."

"But you didn't believe me for a long time. Now you believe me. And it frightens you."

"I cannot authorize a sanction. We do not sanction people."

"I know. It's the reason we had to use boom boxes to attack Noriega in the Vatican embassy in Panama. When all else fails, make noise."

"The business in Panama was botched from the beginning. That wasn't the fault of R Section. The Langley firm fucked up that intelligence. He was their man, not ours."

"But Henry is our man, Hanley, isn't he?"

"What do you want? A piece of paper that says you have been hired by the government of the United States to find and kill Henry McGee, a former employee turned traitor twice?"

"I don't suppose I'd get that."

"What do you want?"

"Authority. A mission directive to the effect that Henry McGee is sought abroad for the attempted assassination of an agent of Section. Named Devereaux. Who is a current employee of Section."

"You want to come back in?"

Devereaux had no pity now in his gray eyes. "No. I want that authority and when I've got him, it'll be done. Then I'll retire on disability as you wanted and spend the rest of my life forgetting the first part of it."

"But it's authority to try to apprehend a suspect—"

"I'll kill him overseas, Hanley. I won't drag the blackbird home and put him on your doorstep. I don't want your approval for this but it's one more thing on my side to have a mission directive in my pocket."

"What will you do with Miss Macklin?"

"That's none of your business, I told you that."

"We didn't mean her harm, Devereaux," Hanley began. Was he apologizing?

"But you did her harm with that quack Krueger. You did her harm, Hanley." Now his voice was low, without any edge to it. "If you had meant her harm, I would have killed you as well."

"You're crazy. You've gone too far. Too many years living by your own rules."

"There are no rules."

God, this room was cold and damp and bleak, exactly like an Irish tavern in the middle of winter. Hanley felt withered to his soul.

"When do you want it?"

"Tomorrow."

"Where will you be?"

"Right here."

"What if Mrs. Neumann vetoes it?"

"Tell her the truth of things if you have to. Or lie to her. It doesn't matter."

"And then you'll quit Section."

"You'll never see me again. Or hear from me. As long as you send my disability checks."

"Government pensions are not great."

"They're sufficient."

"But what will you do?"

Devereaux put down the glass of beer. It was empty. He looked at the foam and then around him, at the walls of gloom and the drawn faces of the morning drinkers. He spoke not for Hanley but for himself.

"Live with Rita Macklin," Devereaux said.

TWENTY-SIX

This is what they said in the office of the magazine on L Street on the morning Mac called in sick for the first time in twenty-two years.

"Mac is sick."

"He hasn't looked good for a long time."

"Christ, do you think it might be serious?"

"He drinks too much. He's an old man. He's going to have to retire anyway. I don't understand how people can let themselves go the way he let himself go. Alcohol is a drug."

"He's an old man."

"He must be sixty."

"So who's going to get his job?"

"They're going to have to fill it out of New York."

"I wish I could move up to New York. I really hate Washington."

163

"Where would you live?"

"I'd like to get a co-op on the East Side. I love that city. It's exciting. I mean, just take Bloomie's. What have you got in Washington to compare with that?"

"Mac goes and then the new man comes in from New York, maybe he can shake this place up. Mac is . . . well, he's just old, you know?"

She pushed strips of toast into the poached eggs on her plate. It reminded her of her mother and of her childhood in Eau Claire, Wisconsin, where the winters were long and hard and the summers were festive because of their brevity. When she had a cold and had to stay home from school, her mother made her poached eggs and buttered toast and cut the toast into strips so that she could play with the eggs, and push the strips into the center of the yolks. Oh, God, she was crying again, sitting at the table in this man's house, and he was staring at her.

"Rita, honey, what's wrong with you?"

She looked up, blinked, saw it was Mac. For a moment, she didn't know where she was. She thought she was home in Eau Claire and she was eight years old. She blinked and wondered why she was sitting in pajamas at a table in front of her boss. My God, why were they in this situation? She had a story to do, a story about something she had forgotten but she probably had it written down in her notes.

"What am I doing here, Mac?"

"Eating breakfast, Rita. Don't you like poached eggs?"

"I had them when I was a child, when I was sick."

"I didn't know that. I just wanted to make you something to eat."

"I'm sorry I cried."

"You can cry anytime, Rita," Mac said.

"I'm feeling . . . strange, Mac. What are we doing here? Where is here?"

"You slept a long time. Fourteen hours. You dreamed a lot and you were shaking and we watched you."

"Who? Dr. Krueger?"

"No. Devereaux. Do you remember he took you from the sanitarium?"

She remembered the man then. She remembered him too much. He never came when she wanted him.

"I feel like I've lost my mind. Sometimes. I just forget things and then I remember other things. Do you understand?"

"Sure," Mac said. "You're in my house. I'm taking a few days off, sick leave. I can take care of you, Rita. He said you'd feel better the longer you were away from the drugs."

"Who? Dr. Krueger?"

"Devereaux."

"He never came to see me."

"He came. He was nearly blown up in his hotel room the night he came. He was in a hospital and they wouldn't let him call you because they thought it would upset you."

She blinked. Her hair was dulled by illness and neglect. It fell in unkempt locks around her face. Her eyes were dull. Her cheeks were thin and the gauntness of her body killed Mac. Devereaux had been right. They were killing her to save her life.

"Eat your eggs, they're good for you."

"Yes," she said. She began to eat the eggs and the toast. She felt sick and tired but better than she had grown accustomed to feeling. Even when she had cried just then, it wasn't a bad thing. She had cried over something sweet in memory, not over a nightmare. There had been too many nightmares, and maybe now she was on the verge of getting rid of them.

Maybe she was going to be all right.

TWENTY-SEVEN

"**D**o you remember?"

She had brushed her hair. She had put on a dress that had belonged to Mac's wife. She sat across from Devereaux and nodded. "I remember going into the parking lot of my building. I was thinking about you, Dev. I was always thinking about you."

They were in the darkened parlor of the town house. Mac was at the grocery up the street. He wasn't used to shopping for groceries; a single man living alone craves company when he dines and his refrigerator begins to resemble an impressionistic painting of single leftovers—a tomato gone bad, a stick of celery uneaten, a bottle of curdled milk.

"I did the wrong thing when I left you. I thought I brought you nothing but trouble and pain. So I left you and brought you nothing but trouble and pain. I won't leave you ever again.''

She said, "I don't believe you."

It was what he feared the most.

"I'm leaving Section. There's one last matter."

"There's always one last matter. That's why I don't believe you."

She thought she looked pretty in the dress. She thought she should buy some lipstick.

"Henry McGee shot you. And tried to kill me. He called me in the hotel the night he blew up the room. He's crazy and he's still in the business of terror. Section wants him taken out as much as I do because he has a trail that goes back to Section. You don't know this because I never told you, I was trying to get away from you."

"Well, you've succeeded," Rita Macklin said. "Did you have fun getting away from me?"

She wanted to hurt him.

"What about women, Dev? You're good-looking. You can have women and you want them. You could seduce them the way you seduced me the first time we met in Florida. You just crept into my mind and sat there until I had to spread my legs for you. I didn't go to bed with men then the way women go to bed with men now. I didn't sleep with men because I felt like it or I had an itch that day or because I was bored or because it seemed a good way to end the evening. I was a good girl, Dev, by the standards of the times. Did you screw me because I was a good girl and that counted for more, to get a good girl?"

He wouldn't answer her; or maybe the silence was answer. She leaned forward.

"You had women when you left me, when you wouldn't call me. I called you and called you and I wanted you. But you were away, screwing women."

"I slept with other women," he said. "That's what you want me to say."

Yes. Exactly what she wanted.

"I slept with other men," she said. "I didn't miss you at all. There was a war correspondent, a wonderful man, we made love and I fell in love with him. Barry. I really loved him."

"What happened to him?"

"He was killed in Nicaragua. Terrorists. Or the government. It didn't matter because he was dead in any case."

"I'm sorry."

"I never missed you. I thought you were dead. I thought they pretended to relay my telephone calls to you because they didn't want anyone to know that an agent had died. They're bastards, spooks. They could do that. They think they can do anything."

"I missed you every day and every night."

"You're a liar. You tell that to all the girls. Girls are made to be lied to."

"I'm not lying to you, Rita."

"You said words lie. I remember that. So if words lie, why are you telling me things? You tell me you'll never leave me but you're going to leave me to find Henry McGee."

"Don't you want me to leave? Then I'll stay. I won't go after Henry McGee. To hell with Section."

They were silent for a long time in the looming darkness of the room. The darkness was palpable because of the edge of light from the moonlit windows. Every object was soft and warm because of the darkness. The room painted their eyes. She saw his eyes, saw the gray so honest that it pained both of them.

"Do you mean it?"

"Yes. I'll quit Section. I don't owe them anymore. And I can leave now because the cold war is over and all the soldiers can go home."

"Will they let you?"

"They'll have to."

"And you'll stay with me."

"Until you're old and gray and don't even want to make love anymore."

My God.

She reached across the darkness and he held her and felt her body beneath the thin satin dress and felt the bones of illness and smelled her sweet breath and the sweet flower odor of her unperfumed skin. She buried her face in his neck and kissed him and felt the wince of pain across his shoulders and let him go.

"I'm sorry, I didn't mean to hurt you," she said.

He reached for her again. He kissed her with the gentleness of yearning. "I love you."

"Don't the words lie anymore?"

"No. Deceit has retired," he said. He held her tightly.

"Oh, Dev. I wanted you all the time. Why didn't you call me?"

"I was running away from you. I thought it was better to hurt you once and for all than to hurt you in little doses all your life. I thought you'd just get fed up and turn your back and forget me."

"I wanted to. I really wanted to. I hated you. You walked out on me and that really hurt. You hurt my pride. I thought my love was worth a lot more. I thought if I loved someone, anyone, they'd have to see they didn't have a chance. They couldn't walk out on me because I loved them.''

And for the first time, she saw the change.

My God, she thought, there are no lies at all.

Because he was crying and he had never done that before.

TWENTY-EIGHT

They did not make love. They lay together in darkness, in her bedroom in the still of midnight in the town house. They were naked next to each other and they saw the wounds on each other. He said he loved her again and she believed him, just as she believed him when he said he would never leave her. She had won him by dying; he had recovered his life by dying. They had both died and awakened in spring. They had no winter left to them. He was no longer November, frozen in time and space across the years in the position of a winter soldier, an agent of violence and silence.

She had wept many times.

Now she was not weeping. They lay in silence, exhausted by all their words to each other.

"Henry McGee," she said.

He turned to her and could see her profile in the lamp of

moonlight that filtered through the curtained window. She was more beautiful than he had ever remembered her, even the first time he had met her on that beach in Florida, even the first time he had tasted of her sweet breath and made love to her body.

"I love you, Dev. You were the only love in my life. Even if I thought I loved another man. Even Barry, who was sweet and gentle and brave."

"It doesn't matter. I'm sorry he died."

"Henry McGee," she said. "I should thank him for shooting me. He brought you back to me."

He saw how bitter it was with her and he couldn't say anything.

She looked at him. "You do love me."

"I always did. I couldn't move, I was frozen away from you."

"The world. It was the world you lived in. You don't have to live in it anymore. It was agents and death and deceit and lies and spies and all of that and you couldn't tell me and you couldn't let me in it."

"No."

"Were you going to arrest Henry McGee? If I let you go?"

"No."

"Were you going to thank him for bringing you to your senses and back to me?"

He didn't know what to say.

"You see, Dev? How I've changed too?"

"Yes. I'm sorry, Rita."

"I know you are. But the hurts are still there."

"Yes."

"If I told you to get out of my sight and leave me alone, would you do that?"

"I told you: I'll never leave you."

"Then you're going to impose yourself again. Like kidnapping me from the sanitarium. I'm not afraid of you. I could put you in jail for a long time. I've got my own life. Or I could let you hang around and just hurt you all the time. Do you know how a woman can do that? There are thousands of ways. You see men being hurt all the time. I could do that to you."

He waited in the darkness.

"It's a bad world, full of bad people," she said.

"Yes."

"Are you bad or good, Dev? I just want to know."

"I don't know what I am."

"You saved that little boy's life on the island that time. You didn't have to do that. Our little black son, Philippe, back home again and working to save his people from themselves."

Devereaux waited.

"That was good," she said in her soft, absent voice. Her voice had changed as well. "Then there's murder. That's always bad, Dev. I told you to kill a man once and you didn't do it at first, not when I told you to kill him. I would have killed him myself. Instead you waited and he hurt me and hurt me and then you finally killed him. Is that it? Did you get some pleasure out of his hurting me that made it more pleasurable to kill him finally?"

He still waited.

She looked at him. Her eyes glittered in the moonlight and her voice was sure, low, coming from the back of her throat and from the pit of her belly. "Let's kill him, Dev. Henry McGee. I want to kill him. You can kill him and I can kill him and then we're really bound. We'll be together, our hands will be dipped into the same pool of blood. Our bond.''

He saw it, saw it in her voice, in her eyes in the moonlight. He saw everything in that moment.

''Yes,'' he said.

''Yes,'' she said, and squeezed his hand.

''We'll kill him.''

TWENTY-NINE

Trevor Armstrong trembled. He had been trembling all night. The police interrogation had made him tremble. The cold man from the government who was probably with SAS had made him tremble. They had penetrated him too roughly. They had taken him apart and left the pieces on a table.

A wooden table in the cellar with an empty vial that smelled of nothing.

"They died but we can't tell how or why. Not yet. Just dead," the government secret agent had said to him. He had a thin, pale face and pale eyes and there might not have been any blood beneath his skin. "The point is—who wanted to kill them? Or did whoever it was want to kill you?"

It was the last thought that frightened him finally. He had expected a strike at the airline, not at himself. Were they insane? What would it profit them if he died? And then he thought of Carl Greengold.

Carl Greengold wanted the airline and Trevor Armstrong was all for letting it happen. Not in so many words, but there it was. Carl Greengold specialized in the Wall Street business of taking companies over and then taking them apart and dispensing the pieces like bits of meat to various other dogs of business war.

How much was Euro-American Airlines worth exactly? There were a certain number of planes, repair shops, real estate, a reservation system, slots in the form of gates owned at key airports in the world. London was key, so was New York. What was the business worth? Trevor Armstrong had figured it out at almost the same time Carl Greengold in New York figured it out: the company was worth more than it cost, in the form of price of shares on the New York Stock Exchange. Be quick in a buyout of the airline and the share prices would still rise but there would still be so much profit left over in taking the airline apart.

But before you tear an airline apart, you milk it. You crush the unions, strip services, skip amenities, fake maintenance, and squeeze all the intangibles out of it. When you've made your money and more, then you make even more by tearing the airline apart.

That's as far as Trevor had gone. He owned forty-one million dollars' worth of stock in EAA and he had borrowed nearly all of the money to buy the shares. He owed back nineteen million. Twenty-two million profit. On paper. At the moment. For the time being.

He poured a glass of Glenlivet and drank it neat. He was

sitting in the parlor of his home, which was now guarded by police. The ambulances were gone. The dead had been taken away to the place where the dead were taken. His dog had been personally buried by his secretary, Jameson, in the garden behind the house. Four dead. Five, counting the dog.

"Have you had any threats, Mr. Armstrong?"

He had shaken his head over and over. He had called Carl Greengold and then canceled the call when he thought about it—what could he tell Carl Greengold that wouldn't drive down the price of EAA in the morning in New York? Terror against an airline, a shaky sort of thing but shaky things were always terrifying the stock market. Especially as Carl Greengold was waiting to buy up the final lots he needed to take the thing over. Wouldn't Carl Greengold like the price of the shares to drop further, even if he lost a little change on the deal? After all, the net worth of the airline was still there. Still so much money. So many planes and jobs and slots to fill.

The fire roared in the fireplace. He could hear the policemen outside his home. They exchanged muffled words with each other, they talked on squawky radios. It was surrealistic.

He thought of his little dog. He would fire his security chief, Dennison, in the morning. No. He couldn't do that. He had to lie low.

Everyone was pledged to keeping this quiet. The secret agent from the British government emphasized this. No one wanted the general public to know that four people had been mysteriously killed in a house in Mayfair by methods not known to the police. Or the government. They suspected some sort of nerve gas but . . . where the hell did terrorists lay their hands on nerve gas? Bombs were so much cheaper and more plentiful. The secret agent didn't say all these things to Trevor, just enough to make Trevor see there was no point in arousing the general public.

Trevor, with trembling hand, again poured whiskey into a glass. He was dealing with a crazy man, he thought. Or he was dealing with Carl Greengold.

He saw it then. Carl Greengold. "Ruthless" was a term overused on the Street but Carl Greengold had once killed a man in his offices in New York, a crazed and desperate man who had lost in a Carl Greengold deal, a fucking nobody and it had been called justifiable homicide before the corpse was cold. But still . . .

Carl Greengold, forty-four years old, had killed a man. That was taking a life, not taking a risk or a contract or taking over a company. Dead was dead.

If it was Carl, then why send a man like that ridiculous Cassidy fellow who pretended to be the FBI to give him a warning?

Trevor saw the logic of his question. He got up from his leather wingback chair and crossed to the mantel and stared into the fire. Bits of oak from a tree that had reached its two hundredth year before being chopped down were burning. Four people had died in his house. He felt sick, sick from whiskey and from dread.

After the police had cleared the house, he had snorted a line of cocaine through a plastic straw in the bathroom under the stairs and then thrown the straw into the fire. The police had been all through the house but they had not discovered the cocaine. Just as well, another fine mess of troubles. The cocaine alerted him to every nuance of the situation but in no way did it make him happy. The whiskey made him dull at the edges and that made him happy now, to have his thought processes slowed.

Dead. People were dead. Servants, but still people.

"Mr. Armstrong."

He turned too abruptly at the sound of the voice. Dennison, chief of security, his face as white as chalk, even in the fiery shadows of this room.

"What do you want?"

"I talked to Jameson when he was burying the dog. I'm sorry about the dog, sir."

"So am I."

"Sir, Jameson said you had a visitor to your office four days ago. An FBI man."

Trevor wished his hand would stop trembling. He wanted to cut it off because it betrayed him.

"What about it?"

"He said . . . the man acted in a peculiar manner and demanded an off-the-record conference with you. You didn't tell me, sir."

"There was nothing to tell you."

"What did he say to you, sir?"

Silence. The fire crackled. The room was alive with dancing ghosts made by shadows and flickering lights.

"Sir?"

"I don't think it concerns you, Dennison."

"If it's related to the security of the airline, sir . . ."

Trevor Armstrong realized he would have to lie to this thick-necked Englishman who was his employee. It grated on him.

"Dennison."

"Sir?"

"What I am about to tell you is in the strictest confidence. I'll relay it to you because Jameson broke a rule about confidentiality and you deserve to be put in the picture. Now."

Trevor cleared his throat.

Dennison waited like a policeman, back on his heels, his hands folded across his lower belly. Respectful and silent and waiting for an answer.

Trevor turned to the fire so that his back was to Dennison.

"My former wife. Allison. As you know, we had a . . . strained divorce. Allison is threatening me now with refusing to let our son visit me. She's removed him from his home and I don't know where he is. This is a painful private matter and I've consulted with the FBI about it. Cassidy from the FBI was . . . there to give me details."

"I see, sir. I'm sorry, sir. It didn't relate to the airline at all."

"Not at all." He turned back to Dennison. The trembling had stopped. "But you understand my wish to keep this matter as confidential as possible. You know now. Even Jameson doesn't know. I appreciate your discretion."

"You have it, sir," Dennison said.

Trevor looked at him closely in the firelight. What did he detect there? A slight change in expression, a certain shifting of the center of the universe. Dennison knew something now that he had not known a moment before, and that gave him leverage suddenly with the boss. Him and the boss. They might have a pint together sometime. A moment before, Dennison thought he might lose his position at any moment; now he knew he wouldn't and that made it different. Trevor saw this in an instant in the slight change of expression on Dennison's potato face, a slightly different cast to his eyes. It angered Trevor but he held his anger. Not now, not now. Not with the world watching, with Carl Greengold watching in New York, not with a potential twenty-two-million-dollar profit waiting to be had. Not now.

THIRTY

There were two persons Maureen Kilkenny had to kill. Henry McGee explained it to her after sex.

The sex was something new for her. Henry kept at it for a long time and she came and came and gulped and sobbed in her coming and dug her fingers into his back and arched her spine and almost screamed. Did scream.

He made her weak with her wanting.

And when it was over and she crawled across his chest to snuggle under his chin, he explained about the killings.

The first was a girl named Marie Dreiser. She was nineteen years old or maybe older, it didn't matter. He described her in loving detail.

"What's she to you then?" Maureen let a jealous note betray her voice.

185

"A piece of ass," Henry said. "Which is what you are at the moment. But you are a fine, fine piece of ass, the best I've had in a long time."

"You bastard," she said, and pushed up, and he hit her. They fought across the bed and he pinned her down, kneeling on her arms. And she bit at his penis and nearly got it.

He pulled back sharply but laughed at the same time.

"Fire. You got belly fire, girl, I like a girl with that."

"I can kill ya," she said.

"I don't want you to kill me, honey. I want to screw you and give you all the money in the world and put you up at the Savoy Hotel and take you out to Connaught's. Or maybe we'll go live in Paris for a while. Or Tahiti. I like Tahiti. It's warm. Would you like to be warm?"

"You're crazy, whoever you are. You talk crazy."

Henry smiled. "I ain't crazy, Maureen. I need you and that's why you're something to me. I didn't know if Irish girls could fuck. You do nice work. I bet you had practice."

She snarled at him.

Henry kept the grin. He was a naked, leering, dark-faced satyr and Maureen saw hellfire around him. For a moment, she cowered on the bed.

"This Marie person is nothing to me," Maureen said.

"I know that, honey. I'll pay for her. Ten thousand and do it neat and soon. The second person you'll do for free."

"I will then?"

"Matthew. Your supreme leader. The man who betrayed you."

"Ah. That's different. That's nothing to you—"

"Honey, you still don't get it. Terror pays. I am talking five million dollars, honey. It could buy you silk underwear thrown away every day. It could buy you any damned thing in the world. Are you so committed to the Irish struggle you wouldn't like to buy your way across the world and ride in limousines and have servants to beat?''

He talked so damned queer. But he kept coming back to the money. And to specifics. Like killing this girl.

"Why don't you kill her yourself?"

Henry shook his head. The hotel room around them was full of dark oak furniture of the nineteenth century and it cost $325 a night. That had impressed Maureen right away, along with the brocaded lobby and the scraping bellboys. Yes. She could learn to live with wealth and power.

"I'd like to. I really would."

She believed him.

"But I got places to go and people to see in the morning. This thing is coming to the flashpoint. Either I get it done now or it don't get done. You kill the bitch and I'll be putting the seal on the deal. Then you kill Matthew O'Day. I want the bastard dead by tomorrow night. Timing is everything.''

"Where's this Marie then?"

Henry saw it. He had her again.

"She's waiting for me in the house off Maida Vale where you interviewed this morning.'' Henry stepped back to the bed and slipped into the sheet. He pulled her to him. He kissed her and it made her crazy again and made her belly start scratching again. God, he was a lover!

And then he stopped just when she wanted him to go on. She rubbed herself against him.

"Go over there and kill her first thing. And then you find Matthew back in that shithouse hotel and you finish him off. And then you come back here, honey, and take a nice bath and slip into bed and wait for me. I should be along around teatime.''

"Then how am I supposed to kill this girl?"

"I'll give her a call. Tell her you're coming and that you're part of the plan. She doesn't understand all of the plan, she thinks this is about using the IRA."

"Is it?"

"Not at all. Matthew O'Day dropped a parcel for me this morning that had a book in it. You both thought it was a bomb. It isn't. Matthew is the fall guy, I told you. I got a set of photographs of him delivering the parcel to a certain house in Mayfair. The thing is: three or four or five folks in that house died shortly afterward."

"Then it was a bomb."

"Bomb, bomb, bomb. You Irish got bombs on the brain. It wasn't a fucking bomb, you stupid cunt. It was a setup. I set up a terrorist named Matthew O'Day because I needed a dead fish to give to the cops when it's time to blow. I don't intend to leave a trail, honey."

She really didn't understand. He suddenly mounted her and penetrated her and the sharpness of the act, the roughness, made her cry out. But that passed in a moment. They made sex again, urgent and demanding, and after a while, he pushed her out of bed and she went down on her knees and she wanted to do it exactly the way he wanted her to do it.

When that was done again, she held him around the waist and looked up at his dark face.

"Jesus, man, you're a fookin' bull," she said.

"I'll fuck you three times a day," he said.

"Why's this girl got to be killed then?"

"She betrayed me," Henry McGee said. "I can't stand that."

"How did she?"

"I can't tell you. Not now. Are you with me, Maureen, or are you too stupid to see your chances?"

He overwhelmed her. She shook her head but she couldn't shake him loose from her. He crawled inside her skin and sat there, warming his hands on her belly fire.

She shook her head again.

"Yes," she said, as she shook her head.

THIRTY-ONE

Devereaux left in the morning. Rita would meet him in three days in the Shelbourne Hotel in Dublin. He said he had to make contacts and move quickly but he said they would both kill Henry McGee, that he would not kill the man without her. It was a promise and she believed him.

Rita felt so very strange.

Mac sat across from her at the chess table in the living room and made a move. He moved his knight to the position where he could take the queen. She saw it and moved the queen away.

Mac took a sip of his whiskey. He drank martinis out, whiskey in. He remembered it had to do with his wife, who liked a tot of whiskey now and then and who thought men should only drink whiskey because it was a man's smell, it

191

had been the smell of her father. He drank whiskey at home for her. Now she was gone and he drank it for her still.

"You can't get away," he said.

She looked at the queen and saw it was true. The rook was behind her, waiting to take her. The knight was before her.

"I give up," she said.

Mac smiled at her. He was so sweet. He had always been so sweet. She had once thought she would let Mac make a pass at her and have her if he did. But he didn't. She knew he had wanted to but he didn't. When was it? The lonely night of her thirty-fifth birthday when she knew Devereaux would never come to see her again. She had loved Devereaux and he had still been able to walk out on her.

She looked at Mac and smiled. "What are you thinking about?"

Mac blinked his eyes to end his reverie. Then he blushed. He actually blushed. "It was nothing. I was thinking about something. Another time. Something about that dress reminded me of something."

"It's a beautiful dress," she said.

"Yes. It is. It's beautiful on you, Rita."

"Oh, Mac."

She understood. She felt so bad and she understood everything in the world, understood Devereaux and the way of all men and their bravenesses and deceits and vulnerabilities. It made her sad to think of it. It made her sad to see Mac blush and end his reverie.

She got up and crossed the carpet to stand next to him. He looked up at her.

She knelt down on the rug and held him and kissed him. She kissed him on the lips and kissed him gently but with wetness and with warmth and with all the wonderful things that a woman can keep in her belly to comfort men on lonely mornings.

There was rain against the windowpanes. Washington shivered at the end of fall. The fall was so long and soft and lingering in Washington that you began to believe sometimes that the fall would never end, that there would just be this falling and falling through the colors on the trees in the Virginia hills all around, that fall would be like life and go on and on despite the common belief that all things ended. And then there was rain like this and it reminded you of the end of things and made you lonely.

He said, "I don't want to hurt you, Rita. I really love you. I would do anything for you."

"You've done everything," she said.

"You. And him," he said. He shook his head.

"No," she whispered. "Me. Me."

"I thought of her. I thought of a time when she wore that dress at a party. The magazine or something. We were in the ballroom at the Willard. It was a cocktail party and I hurried over from work and when I saw her, it was a new dress, I just loved her and we didn't even go home, we went upstairs to the corporate suite and we made love on the bed, in our clothes, made love without even taking the sheets out, just as if we were young."

"Then make love to me," Rita Macklin said.

"No. That would be wrong—"

"No. It would be wrong the other way," she said. "I love you, Mac, I really do."

"You love him."

"Yes."

"You can't—"

"Yes," she said. "Yes I can."

"Rita," he protested one last time. But she took his hand and he had to rise with her and follow her. In the morning bedroom where the bed lay unmade, she turned and kissed him again, sure of herself, pulling his head to her lips and letting the smell of herself fill this room and empty space in him. He touched her as she wanted to be touched. He slipped his hand down the satiny flesh of the dress to her lower back and lower and held her and she pressed against him, gaunt and bony and not sick at all anymore but filled with sunshine and pity for the world that endured darkness and hardness.

"Rita," he said to catch his breath.

"Do it now," she said, pulling him to the sheets. She opened her legs for him and the dress rode up her thighs and he fumbled and found her and he fell upon her, consumed her with his kisses. Touches. Love.

THIRTY-TWO

But he didn't go to Dublin after all.

Hanley told him the morning scan as they rode to Dulles for the Concorde Air France flight to Paris. It would be faster to reach Ireland from Paris than to wait for the usual nighttime flight of Aer Lingus.

"Tell me."

"British intelligence has a murder on their hands. Actually, four murders. Four people all struck dead in a town house in Mayfair yesterday. But the Brits can't figure out why or how and don't want to panic the public by saying there might be a secret nerve gas or something being used to kill innocent people in the heart of London."

The Lincoln limousine was not to Hanley's style or liking but this was a matter of security. The driver behind the partition was cleared to the level of N inside Section. The automobile was secured against eavesdropping devices by constant static produced by three amplifiers around the passenger compartments. The tires were puncture proof.

"And this links to Henry McGee?"

"I remembered something. I spent two hours going back through computers and I really am not that expert at it. I brought in Mrs. Neumann and told her what I thought I had remembered. There is so much to remember and most of it is junk and it just piles up in the brain and—"

"Tell me," Devereaux said. They were in the sprawl of Virginia suburbia now; there were signs of Dulles International flashing by.

"Four weeks ago. In Naples. Our naval intelligence people have been helping on the investigation of the bombing of Flight One forty-seven. You remember, you were conscious then, it was in the papers—"

"The Euro-American Airlines plane," Devereaux said. "That's a cheerful thought to bring up on the way to the airport."

Hanley frowned. "The point is, they were eyeballing a Mediterranean arms dealer who goes by the name of Juno. Juno has all kinds of contacts, all kinds of people he deals with. He's strictly For Sale. Well, the NI people were eyeballing him constantly and they happened to record a meeting he had with an American. They put out the description on him but it zipped right by me. I didn't connect. They had a photograph even but if you didn't call it up on computer, you didn't get it. Today, I called it up. NI wasn't interested in the man Juno was talking to; they were interested in getting as much information about Juno as they could to see if he was involved in the terror bombing of Flight One forty-seven."

"Was he?"

"Nobody knows. I think it's a case of nobody wanting to know very much. If it's Libya, what are we going to do again, bomb Gaddafi or his children?"

"Who was Juno meeting in Naples?"

"Henry McGee."

"And what transpired?"

"Juno gave him a bottle of vodka. Smirnoff."

"Is that what they think?"

"They saw it with their own eyes."

"And four people were killed in a house in London with no apparent causes."

"You didn't ask me whose house it was."

Devereaux smiled at Hanley. "You're getting interested in this finally."

Hanley had betrayed eagerness. He shook it off. It wasn't like him to have enthusiasm. "Trevor Armstrong. Chief executive for Euro-American Airlines. I ran him through the routine and they're still looking at him in New York. The point is, what is the connection between the IRA terrorism and the murder in that pub and the blowing-up of a Euro-American plane? I mean, what's the connection?"

"Is that rhetorical, Hanley? Are you really that dense?"

"I had to dance carefully with Mrs. Neumann. I needed her help but I couldn't explain the thing fully. About you. I signed the mission directive myself. She wouldn't have approved."

"No. She wouldn't have," Devereaux said. He took the piece of paper, unfolded it, read it, and folded it again. He put it in his breast pocket.

"Terrorism. I don't understand it," Hanley said. "There has to be some profit motive."

"Keep on checking Trevor Armstrong and anything else to do with stock purchase at EAA," Devereaux said. "Maybe

197

that's what it's about. Maybe the airline is being targeted by Henry.''

"But why kill a houseful of servants of the CEO?"

"To terrorize him," Devereaux said. "To shake a money tree.''

"I'll have to tell Mrs. Neumann in time—"

Devereaux said, "How much time?"

Hanley said, "Damnit. When I tell her I authorized a mission, she'll—"

"She'll jump all over you. Wear rubber clothing. You could tell the Brits now and they'd pick Henry up and make him sing. We don't want that, do we?"

"No."

"But would Mrs. Neumann be able to see it through? Leave it alone, Hanley, leave me alone. I can get you out of this."

"By killing Henry McGee."

"And everyone else who was in it with him," Devereaux said.

THIRTY-THREE

"Hello," Henry McGee said.

"Where are you?" Marie said. She was sitting at the kitchen table in the back of the rented apartment off Maida Vale. She wore a robe and she had smoked half a package of Marlboro cigarettes. Her voice was husky from the smoke.

"Up to no good," Henry said, putting a smile in his voice. "You did good, honey, the pictures turned out nice. The thing is that in the next forty-eight hours, we got to put the setup nicely, nicely. In an hour or so, the girl from the IRA cell, Maureen, she's gonna show up at the flat. Let her in and then the two of you wait. I should be able to hit the target before noon if I get any luck at all."

"What does she look like?"

"Got real dark red hair. Irish-looking."

"Sure," Marie said.

"Bye, honey, I gotta run," Henry said, like any harried businessman on the ride to the commuter station.

She heard the click.

She got up and stretched. Then she thought about the girl who was coming to this flat. She went down the hall into a bathroom and took a quick shower. She dressed again in her black jumpsuit. She brushed her short, tough-bristled hair and looked at herself. She wasn't very pretty but what the hell.

She went into the hall back to the kitchen.

She turned on the electric kettle to make tea. The kitchen was deadly white, very clean and ugly like a hospital room. She moved around the kitchen doing things while the water heated. When it was boiling, the kettle clicked sharply. She poured the water over tea bags in a porcelain pot called a Brown Betty. The morning was coming slowly because this was November and London was very far north in the world.

She hummed to herself, she didn't know what the song was.

She opened a cupboard and took out the envelope again. The second set of prints. She studied her handiwork and then put the prints back in the envelope. She didn't know why she had done this, made another set of prints. Henry McGee had killed all those people in the public house that day he went to the west of Ireland. She had known it a moment before she ordered the prints. She suddenly was sure that Henry McGee was insane and that it would be a great danger to her to be close to him.

She went to the refrigerator and opened it, looking for milk. And then she saw it.

A bottle of Smirnoff vodka.

This was very strange.

Henry McGee had purchased a bottle of Smirnoff vodka sometime during the day yesterday when she was out taking photographs of Matthew O'Day. And then he had opened it because the seal was broken.

She stood very still and looked at the bottle and remembered she had seen this bottle before, when they had stayed in the Excelsior in Rome, when she had noticed it in his suitcase. It hadn't been there before he went to Naples and then it was there. She said she wanted a drink and he had gotten very angry and said she was to keep her fucking hands off that bottle and he had slapped her for good measure.

The same bottle.

She stared at it for minutes. And then she saw the second thing.

A small glass jar full of caviar. Black and rich. She loved caviar. Vodka and caviar.

Except it wouldn't be caviar.

She opened the caviar jar and smelled it and she had smelled that before, it was something, something . . .

She spooned the caviar on a plate and saw the small radio, as small as a nine-volt battery, concealed in the bottom of it. Caviar and vodka.

She took out the bottle of vodka and opened it. She sniffed it. It was odorless and vodka is not odorless.

Marie was very afraid now. Henry had killed all those people and he was going to kill her. She didn't know how but she knew it now.

THIRTY-FOUR

Henry McGee sat with the transmitter in his left hand and the steering wheel in his right. The car was a Peugeot with the steering wheel on the English side. He was on a side street in Maida Vale. He had dropped off Maureen a couple of minutes earlier. Maureen would be edging her way around Marie now, thinking about how she was going to do it. Maureen had a knife and she said it was all she needed because she was very strong and it sounded like this German girl was small and not strong.

Henry chuckled at that and pushed the transmitter button. The receiver would ignite the pearls of gelignite dyed black in a caviar jar and available from a merchant in Paris who dealt in such things. Matthew O'Day had gotten that for him. Matthew was proving to be very, very handy for Henry. A good terrorist with good sources could be extremely useful, Henry thought.

By now, the interior of the refrigerator would be around sixteen hundred degrees Fahrenheit and the bottle of nerve gas would have been transformed from a liquid to a gas. It would be filling the apartment while the two girls danced around each other and decided about each other. Shit. There was nothing to decide. They were both dead now. And when their bodies were found in five or six or seven days, the cops would be just as puzzled as they were by the deaths in Mayfair, but by then they would have their suspect. The usual suspect. The stage Irishman in the form of Matthew O'Day with photographs and murder written all over his face.

Damnit. He was clever. He needed the girl Maureen to link the dead bodies in Mayfair with the dead bodies they'd find here with Matthew O'Day. And that would link back to the bombings in the west of Ireland. It might take the authorities some weeks to figure it all out but they'd figure it out. Matthew O'Day had one final mission to do for Henry. And he didn't know it yet. But the cops would link everything to O'Day finally, the dead servants, the dead girls, everything. It all went back to the photographs. And it might take them a while longer to figure out about how all this linked to Trevor Armstrong and EAA but they would. By then, it wouldn't matter. Trevor couldn't tell them anything without compromising himself and Henry would be fucking Polynesian girls in Tahiti.

He dropped the transmitter on the seat and put the car in gear.

In the cold morning light, the Peugeot crept away, down the street that was still waiting to wake up.

THIRTY-FIVE

D evereaux walked through the green line that had a
sign reading NOTHING TO DECLARE. A customs officer stopped
him anyway.

"Will you open that bag, sir?"

Devereaux opened it.

He was in London at last and he was tired. It was night
already, as though daylight had been an afterthought or a
momentary illusion.

The customs officer, wearing British blue and a stiff,
starched collar, plumped through the clothing as though feeling his way around a woman. He ran his hands along the
sidewalls of the bag with a sensual, even lascivious gesture.
He smiled at Devereaux as he did this and Devereaux did not
return the smile.

"Are you here on pleasure, sir?"

"My lifelong dream was to be in London in November," Devereaux said.

The agent frowned.

"Business. I'm a stockbroker." He took out a card and showed him. The agent read the card. He frowned again but had lost interest in the matter.

"Will you be here long, sir?"

"Three days, I think."

"All right, sir. You can close the bag."

Like all competent customs officials, he had managed to disarrange the contents of the bag just enough to make instant closure impossible. Devereaux struggled briefly and the customs official frowned at him for holding up the line. He finally snapped the bag shut and carried it through.

Heathrow was its throbbing, messy self, full of announcements, people of every color, and the din of travel noise that is the most tiresome thing in the world. He found a bank of public phones and went to them. He punched in numbers that connected him to a telephone in a town house in Washington.

"Yes," Mac said.

"Me."

"Do you want her?"

"Yes."

"Just a moment."

Devereaux wondered what he had just heard in Mac's voice. Or in her's, now that she picked up the receiver and spoke into it.

"Dev."

"I'm in London. I think you'll meet me here. And I don't think there's as much time as we thought there would be."

She caught her breath.

"Rita?"

"I'll come on the night plane from Dulles. British Air is seven P.M., I think."

"All right. Check in at Connaught's; I'll contact you. I might not be able to wait. There's been a change. Henry is in London if we're close enough to getting him as I think. It complicates things. I have to set it up differently."

"Dev."

"What?"

"Nothing."

He waited.

"I love you," Rita said.

He waited.

"Dev?"

"What?"

"Dev. I . . . I can't kill him. Not like this. Not in the way it has to be done."

He let his breath out slowly.

"Dev?"

"I know," he said.

"Are you going to kill him?"

"Yes."

"For us?"

"Yes."

"For R Section. You're doing it because it's a thing you've done before. For R Section. You couldn't kill to protect me that once."

He waited some more. The din of Heathrow took the heart out of him. It came on him so suddenly that he felt a pain across his chest that fell into his belly. So tired, so goddamned tired. The pains of his body fell away. It wasn't pain but just this overwhelming fatigue. He might even let the telephone receiver drop from his hand. He might lie down and never rise. He might sleep and never awake. He was suddenly so tired of everything. The man who was tired of London and was tired of life. Was he that man?

He opened his eyes and looked around him and felt sick to his stomach in the same way he had felt sick to his stomach all the time in the hospital when the drugs took over his body and put his mind on the shelf to watch his body from afar.

He was holding a telephone. He wondered why.

"Hello," he said.

"I thought we were disconnected."

He blinked. He knew that voice.

"Hello?"

"Dev. Are you all right?"

"Rita?"

"Dev? Where are you?"

He looked around him. Two Indian gentlemen, their heads wrapped with scarves, passed in Western dress, carrying briefcases and followed like children by two plump Indian ladies in veils and jewels. A gaggle of Japanese businessmen, dressed in identical navy blue suits, followed their leader, who was as lost as they were. Everyone was very lost and time was not on any side but its own. It was like a bazaar of the world.

"I don't know," Devereaux said.

"You're in London."

He remembered that now.

"Dev. Come home. Come home. I need you, you need a doctor now, we're both ill and—"

"Rita. Where are you?"

"I'm at Mac's house. You remember that."

Mac. He had to remember that. M. A. C. There might be questions later. Will this be on the exam? My God, an exam is nothing more than self-knowledge. God, he was tired of them and their empty minds refusing to be filled and he longed to fill himself with the honeycomb of Asian fields beneath the sweltering Asian sky that always warmed him, always filled the fields with rain in monsoon and the fine, hard rain falling warmly down his skin as he walked the muddy tracks through the jungle, endless jungle, sounds of endless gunfire and endless chops of choppers clotting the sky and chopping at nothing . . .

"Dev!"

Rita sounded hysterical.

"What's wrong, Rita?"

"Dev. Dev. You blanked out on me there. You just blanked out. Are you all right? Dev, come back, it's not worth it."

"I'm going to kill Henry McGee. Wait for me, Rita. It'll be just a little time and then I'll come back and I'll never leave you—"

"Love, you just blanked out. What if you do that when you're against Henry? Come back to me, you promised me—"

"Just a little while, Rita. I love you. I always did," he said.

"Dev."

"I love you," he whispered, to silence her.

"Dev."

But he had to leave her now, even though he had promised never to do it.

THIRTY-SIX

"Y es, Miss Turnbull?"

"Mr. Cassidy on the telephone, sir."

Trevor punched button five.

"Yes?"

"This is Mr. Cassidy. Regarding our previous conversation, I wonder if we could have a bit of a chinwag, say, round about noonish."

"Yes." Dull voice, dull eyes. He'd have to cancel his luncheon. "Where?"

The preposterous British accent continued, "Say, my club. No. Come to think of it, they're closed for remodeling. Say, noon at Chester's in the City, do you know it?"

"Noon," Trevor Armstrong said.

"Splendid. And do try to be alone, old bean. Ta-ta then."

Click.

For a long moment, Trevor sat alone in the world. Then the world intruded and Jameson said, "Something?"

"No. Cancel my luncheon with Lord Asbury; a . . . private matter has come up. And send in Dwyer."

Jameson permitted himself the trace of a frown. His employer had any number of "private matters" that would occur during the day and invariably they involved discreet women who were suddenly available for a slap and tickle. Trevor would suddenly put the business on hold for a couple of hours in the Connaught or Dorset with a Miss or Mrs. or Lady and Jameson was expected to provide a suitable cover. He was a man who endured humiliations for the sake of employment, a latter-day Cratchit, but it galled him nonetheless. And sending for the toady Dwyer proved the nature of the something that had come up.

Thirty seconds later, Dwyer was alone in the big room with the boss. Dwyer was fifty, born and raised in Queens, a sharp-faced Irishman with heavy eyebrows and ruddy cheeks. He looked like he was made to wear a green suit and play the leprechaun in a New York Saint Patrick's Day parade.

"Are the police still following me?" Trevor began.

"Yeah. Two of them. They're downstairs now, one in the lobby and one in a car."

"I have a luncheon meeting. I don't want to be followed."

Dwyer knew about Trevor's luncheons. This wife or that one and they'd have tea and sympathy in the Dorset for a nooner with the boss. Sometimes Dwyer would pick them up afterward and take them to their cars or homes and he would judge the success of the boss's courtship on the look on their faces. When they looked dizzy and disheveled and happy, Dwyer figured the boss did good.

"I'll bring the car around to the mews entrance at eleven-twenty," Dwyer began. "We goin' to the Dorset?"

"No." Trevor smiled. "A real luncheon this time. At Chester's in the City. I just don't want to be followed. But I want you to mark who I have luncheon with. He's a man I don't like."

Dwyer found a toothpick in his shirt pocket and slipped it between his lips.

"What do you want me to do?"

"Follow him afterward. I'll make it back to the office on my own. I want to know about this man. And be careful, Dwyer."

"I'm always careful," Dwyer said. "What's it about? Allison and the divorce?"

Trevor nodded. "Yes. About that." He was already thinking about the strange thing he would tell the man who called himself Cassidy.

The dining room was crowded, elbow to elbow, across white tablecloths. Men in livery moved about the place, and ceiling fans shoved the air back and forth. This was lunch at the highest level and no more pleasant than eating Scotch eggs in a Wapping public house over a pint of beer. In fact, considerably less pleasant.

Henry McGee smiled at Trevor Armstrong as he sat down.

"I'm followed everywhere by the police. Ostensibly for my protection. They'll take a look in here and see you."

"Who gives a fuck," Henry McGee said. His mean, dark face showed enjoyment. "I just wanted to see if you were as smart as everyone says you are. I guess you are."

"What does that mean?"

"It means I don't have to kill you. Make a mess on the

tablecloth. If you'd walked in here with cops, I'd have killed you. Funny thing about getting killed by someone, sometimes you don't figure you're only a gesture away from getting it." Grinned.

"Why did you kill those people in my home?"

"Get your attention. How many were there?"

"You didn't know?"

"Story didn't get into the papers. Not yet anyway. Sort of thought that would happen."

"Four servants. And my dog, Jameson."

"Funny name for a dog."

"Look. I don't have five million. Not even close."

"That's too bad. I guess the next thing is to kill your entourage. Or maybe take out the next flight to New York. Two crashes in two months is two too many."

Henry was still grinning, the waiters were rushing around on crepe soles, the dining room hummed with voices pitched at the low, confidential level of the City, and Trevor Armstrong knew his face had turned white.

"Can I deal with you or are you just crazy?" Trevor said at last. The voice was steady; it was borrowed from a reserve that he would have to pay back later in the form of six double whiskeys or two lines of cocaine.

"What's the deal?"

"You can ruin EAA. I admit it." He sighed. He wiped his hands on the napkin on his lap. "Look here. For five million dollars, I'd want more than to be left alone."

"Being left alone after what's happened ought to be enough," Henry McGee said. "Like the surgeon who does a triple bypass. All he guarantees for all that pain and agony is that you're going to be able to take a walk, something you took for granted before."

"Jesus."

Henry was enjoying himself. "Jesus reminds me of what Lazarus said when Christ raised him from the dead. 'Jesus. Why the hell did you do that?' "

"I can get you two million by Friday. And the three million if you'll perform a service."

Henry stared at Trevor. He waited.

"The service is simple. In your line. To get the police away from me and on to another target."

Henry let the silence drift in a sea of voices between them. The waiter came up. They both ordered whiskeys as aperitifs. The waiter announced the special of the day and departed. The din continued around them like perpetual ringing in the ears.

"What do you want?" Henry McGee said.

Trevor had been thinking about it all morning. It was linked with thoughts of Carl Greengold and what eventual effect the deaths in his house would have on the price of EAA. The police would leak the story eventually; there were always leaks. And would it be before or after Carl Greengold made his move and the price of EAA started going through the ceiling? It was all about money, the money borrowed to buy stock and the volatile price of the stock itself.

"A bombing," Trevor Armstrong said. He stared at Henry with steady eyes. "We have strong rivals for this market."

Henry said, "You are a murderous bastard." Grinned again. "You got anyone in mind? Or is this just spin the bottle?"

"Another airline. It'll work to your advantage as well." The words were rushing up and Trevor couldn't stop them. "Muddy the trail. You know the police will eventually settle on you and your . . . colleagues. Wouldn't it serve to your advantage to diffuse the trail by diffusing the target?''

Henry accepted his whiskey. They ordered salads without enthusiasm and the waiter departed.

"Cheers," Henry said and sipped.

Trevor did not touch his whiskey. He stared at Henry McGee.

"The thing is, that's more work than I intended to do."

"And you never believed you'd get five million dollars either," Trevor said. He was very cold now, sure of himself, negotiating with the head of the pilots' union or facing down a hostile board member. His manner had altered because he had proposed a deal and a deal was something he could understand. Everything before—the mindless terrorism—had panicked him.

Henry sipped the whiskey again. He rarely drank and almost never in the middle of the day but he was coming to the end of something and this was a celebratory moment. The deal was concrete, something to touch and figure out about. Trevor was a little more man than he had expected.

"I don't know why I have to agree to anything," Henry said.

"Nor I."

"Because you're up to your asshole in debt."

"How the hell do you know so much about me?"

"Because I do my homework, Trev. Because I spent some money and time finding out about you and your buying all that EAA stock. You don't have that kind of money so it stands to reason you borrowed it. And if EAA starts dropping its planes out of the sky, the stock will go down the toilet and you'll be drowning in your own shit. Is that clear to you? It is to me."

"I want a deal and I need a deal. You've put the police on me, they watch me, they want to know what it is about me that someone wanted to murder my household staff. You have to give me room to breathe. If EAA gets hit again, certain . . . people might get panicked and pull out of the market. That wouldn't be a good thing. A good thing would be to have someone else blown up in the way EAA was blown up and shift the cops onto another trail. And it's more than police, I can assure you. A man from a ministry I never heard of was there to question me the night I found . . . those bodies."

Henry looked at his fingertips on the tablecloth. There was a certain amount of sense in all this. Trevor was in a bad spot and he might just be stubborn enough to hold back on the blackmail if Henry didn't go along with his deal. Henry really didn't have time; the whole thing was a matter of exquisite timing and so far it had worked, right down to setting off the remainder of the poison gas in his own flat and killing the two girls.

"I want the money in fifties and hundreds," Henry McGee said. "In a suitcase."

"My God, do you know how much money that is?"

"Divide it this way: a million and a half in American green; a million and a half in pounds sterling; the rest in Swiss francs. Nothing else. And don't cheat me because I won't count it until later and if you cheat me, I'll kill you. Just kill you. And you know that I will."

"It'll take me time—"

"Sell some of your stock. Take wire transfers from your

217

bank account in New York. Get cash out of the corporation. If it comes down to it, put the tap on your chauffeur, just get the money. I don't want paper, I don't want big bills, and I don't take American Express.''

"But time. I need time.''

"Seventy-two hours. Noon on Friday,'' Henry McGee said. "You're a bright man. You'll figure out how to do it.''

"Noon on Friday? That's impossible.''

"There's a plane out of Heathrow at two P.M. for Chicago nonstop. On your friendly rival airline. Is that right, Trevor?''

It was exactly right. Despite himself, he felt drawn to the other man in that moment. The deal was that much closer.

"Now what if I had a passenger aboard that plane who was carrying a parcel? Unknown to him, of course?''

"Who would it be?''

And Henry drew a photograph from his pocket. It was a photograph he had intended to turn in to the SAS but this way was even better. Even neater. Henry prided himself on thinking fast.

It was a photograph of Matthew O'Day delivering a parcel to the house in Mayfair.

Trevor held his breath a moment.

"D'you remember the parcel? A copy of the novel that the movie *Halloween Heaven* was based on? That's Matthew O'Day. He's your friendly neighborhood IRA terrorist and if the British thought this was all about the IRA, it would steer them in a very different direction, don't you think?''

"Yes,'' Trevor managed.

"Matthew can be on that two P.M. flight to Chicago. I can arrange that. I can even arrange a reason why. The point is, when you see Matthew go through the boarding gate, you're gonna be carrying a bag yourself, one for me with five million beans in it. If there's a fuckup, any kind of double cross from you, then the photographs—including the one you just put your fingerprints on—go to SAS and you'll be up shit creek.''

''Matthew O'Day is working for you?''

''Reluctantly, but then, good help is hard to find these days.''

''But what if I do see Matthew O'Day get on that plane? I only have your word that something is going to happen. What if you cross me?''

Henry smiled. ''Now we're getting somewhere, Trevor. A Mexican standoff. I want the bag and you want the bomb to go off on the other guy's plane. But in this case, you got to trust me because you got nothing else. I don't even have to agree to this deal except I can see the logic of it from your point of view. If I push you too far, then you just turn into an ole porcupine and roll up into a ball. I ain't stupid, Trevor, I see that. But if you push me too far, I'll just have to fuck you so you walk funny for the rest of your life. See the way it is? A certain amount of trust has to go on.''

''The police are always following me—''

''Shit. You must think I got shit for brains. I was outside the EAA office this morning at eleven-twenty when you left out the back way, down that mews with your driver. I know the cops ain't following you. You think I leave everything to chance?''

''You called me. They might have tapped my phone—''

''You know and I know you're too smart a businessman to have your phones tapped by the cops. You probably swept them the next morning to make sure. You don't want the cops knowing all your secrets.''

''You really mean this, don't you?'' Trevor stared at the

other man as though seeing him for the first time. His instincts as a man of business and finance took over; he saw the depth of Henry McGee, even if he still did not know his name.

"Nothing complicated, Trevor. I don't want to leave a trail. The only guy I'm leaving behind is you and you're not gonna tell anyone anything because you got your own secrets. So at the end of the world or the war, you and me are the only guys standing. What do you say?"

"Friday at two P.M."

"That's it. We'll wave our Irish friend good-bye as he heads toward America and you and me will check out your luggage."

"And the photographs. I want the photographs. And the negatives."

"That sounds fair," Henry McGee said.

"This is a very delicate moment," Trevor said in a cool voice. His voice was soft but it was there, in all the modulated tones, the voice of a hard man. "I don't want a misstep. I can't afford it."

"You can't and I can't. I think that's the way it goes. Reminds me of a story about this guy hit by the cardinal's limousine. Archbishop of New York. He goes to a hospital, he gets well, but he says he's paralyzed."

"I really think we've concluded this conversation—"

Henry touched his sleeve, then leaned forward across the table and spoke barely above a whisper. "I wanna finish my story."

Henry held his sleeve. His hand weighed a thousand pounds.

Trevor felt pinned to the tablecloth at the wrist. He was staring at terror, pure and simple. He knew Henry could do it, could send a man aboard an airplane carrying a bomb he didn't know about.

"So he sues the archdiocese and it goes to court and the lawyers for the cardinal can't get anything on the guy, even though they know he's faking his paralysis. They hire detectives and everything. The jury finally awards the guy fifty million dollars and there he is, strapped to a board in the courtroom. So the lawyer for the cardinal says to him, 'You won the fifty mill but we're gonna watch you all the time, day and night, and if you slip, we'll put you in jail. So what good is the fifty mill to you, strapped to this board? What are you gonna do with it?'"

"I have to—"

Henry said, "The guy says, 'I'm gonna get a flight to Paris and then charter a car to Lourdes. And when I get there,' he says to the cardinal's lawyer, 'I'm gonna pray for a miracle.'"

Henry removed his hand from Trevor's sleeve. The waiter brought the salads and stood with an enormous pepper grinder under one arm, ready for service.

"Please," Trevor said, and the waiter ground black specks over the creamy sauce.

The waiter looked at Henry McGee.

Henry shook his head. "You got any horseradish?"

The waiter stared at him for a moment before going to fetch the horseradish.

"I like that story," Henry said. He stared hard at Trevor. "Haven't told it for years. You see the point, Trevor? Story should have a point. The delicate moment here is on both sides. You don't want to fail because of what I can do and I don't want to fail because it would complicate things for me. I don't want to push you too far. So I'm giving you a way out and you're giving me what I want and everyone is going to be happy.''

Trevor stared at him.

''Except for the poor schmucks who decided to take that plane to Chicago on Friday,'' Henry said, and chuckled.

THIRTY-SEVEN

This is what happened four hours before Henry's meeting with Trevor Armstrong.

The bell to the flat off Maida Vale rang. Shrill and long. Marie padded to the door in stocking feet and pushed aside the gauze curtain. She saw the red-haired Irish girl through the glass panel. She was wearing a light raincoat. She did not see the Peugeot up the street. Gloomy morning made the street beyond the door dingy.

Marie opened the door and stepped back, as though expecting an attack. She didn't know what she expected. Not from the moment she had found the Smirnoff bottle in the refrigerator and the radio receiver hidden in a jar of caviar. Or whatever it was. She only knew Henry had sent this girl to her. She only knew that Henry did not intend for her to live very much longer.

"Me name's Maureen, I'm from him. You were expecting me?" The last words turned on a high note and it sounded like a question and maybe it wasn't.

"I don't know if I should be expecting you," Marie Dreiser said. The little rat girl was dressed in a plain black jumpsuit that covered her thin frame in an unflattering way. She knew what she was, had always known she was nothing, just a thing, and she had chosen to wear the jumpsuit for this meeting because she wanted everyone in the world to know she was just nothing. So why was it worth Henry McGee's trouble to use her and not discard her but actually kill her? It made her angry with Henry for the first time. She wasn't worth killing and if her life was all she had, then Henry shouldn't take the last thing left in the world.

They stood in the entryway, unmoving. The door was open.

"You're lettin' the chill in," the Irish girl said.

Marie stared at her for a moment. The girl was taller and heavier than Marie but that didn't bother her. Marie had survived all these years—what was it, nineteen or twenty or twenty-one years?—and she would survive longer. Henry McGee was a man and she had survived men. Even loved one man who was too weak to survive. Even been saved by one man who was as strong as she was. If Marie could survive in a world of men, she wouldn't be afraid of any woman.

Marie brushed past the girl to close the door. Then she turned to Maureen.

"What do you do for Henry? Do you kill for him or do you fuck for him?"

A latent sense of guilt and Catholicism blushed Maureen's face.

Marie smiled. "Or both? Do you do both for him? He'd

like that. Just remember the day comes when you're used up and then he'll send you away by final means.''

"I don't understand a word you're saying."

"Didn't I use good English?'' Marie was grinning at the Irish girl, putting her on the defensive, advancing a foot, standing very close to her. Her voice growled and grated, the sound of a sewer beast driven to a corner of the underground and unable to escape. "I know everything and I know you've come to kill me and I want to know if you're doing it because he fucked you so good or because you're being paid for it.''

"Jesus," Maureen said. She took a step back. This was too close. She had only used the knife once before, and that time on a British soldier who had wandered off into the wrong part of Belfast. That time, that night in Belfast, he had fondled her and kissed her and when he closed his eyes to remember the girl he left behind, she had cut his throat and been greatly surprised by all the blood that came out all of a sudden. But at least he was a bloody soldier, not just a girl, someone she didn't even know, someone she had to execute to fulfill her rite of passage. This was too close.

"Come on, love, don't you want a cup of tea before we get down to it?''

The maniac was grinning at her and Maureen took another step back, wary and hesitant, feeling in her coat for the knife.

"Is it a gun or a knife? The Irish always use guns, don't they? But I'm too close, aren't I?"

The German girl took another step and now she pulled Maureen to her. Her strong hands were locked around Maureen's arms and Maureen was surprised at the strength in the little body.

"What are ya doin', girl?''

"Give me a kiss," the rat girl said. "Just a little one before we have to do what we have to do. What Henry wants us to do."

Maureen shook her head.

And the rat girl, grinning, pressed her lips upon Maureen's face and bit her lips. The blood began to foam and run. Maureen cried out and struggled back and still the little girl held on, her arms like steel wires, cutting her circulation. She felt the knife handle in her pocket but there was no way to draw it out.

"Come on, *liebchen*, let's dance down the corridor and maybe I'll kiss you again. Did Henry want us to kiss each other? But no, Henry wouldn't have thought of that. He just thought his little rat girl was going to wait for him and his new lover and meekly go to slaughter with the lambs."

"You're crazy, you are, lemme go now—"

And still Marie held her and pushed her down the hallway, bumping into the walls of the narrow passage. "I'm leading you, Maureen, do you like to dance? I know the music." And she laughed a little shrieking laugh, her manic eyes glittering in the soft light of morning that edged the darkness.

Maureen twisted in her grip and tried to pull her arms away and, finally, burst the grip.

Marie shoved her the final few feet into the kitchen. The lights were all on. There was a cup of tea on the table and a Brown Betty pot. Maureen hit the edge of the table, felt the knife, drew it out. Suddenly, there was six inches of steel between the two women.

And Marie laughed.

The knife was held straight out and rock steady. Maureen narrowed her eyes and tasted the blood on her lips.

"You're crazy," she said.

"And you came to kill me. That doesn't make me the only crazy one, does it? Why do you want to kill me? Is Henry going to make you rich? Are you doing it for the money, love? Don't bother. Henry McGee takes and takes, he doesn't ever give. It's the thing I like about him, the reason I put up with him. He is so simple. Really simple. He thinks I didn't understand but I always understood. Women do. Don't you understand?"

"I understand you, you're a crazy woman—"

"What of it? Are you afraid of me because I'm crazy? Or because that knife isn't enough defense for you? Sit down and have a cup of tea; you've got time before you kill me." And laughed again.

Maureen edged back, she didn't know why; she had the knife but she had to retreat from this strange creature.

"When do you think Henry is going to have you killed?"

"No one's gonna kill me."

Marie was still smiling in a particularly mad way, moving toward the kitchen counter. She reached for an envelope and flung it on the table. "Take a look, love, take a good look at things as they really are."

"I don't want to look at nothin'," she said.

"Look."

Maureen kept her eyes on Marie and reached for the envelope with her left hand. She spilled out photographs on the table.

Photographs of Matthew delivering the parcel to the house in Mayfair.

She looked up. "Where did you get these?"

"I took 'em," Marie said. "I'm his photographer. He wanted one set of prints but I made two. In fact, I went back to the house in the evening. Do you know what happened?

Four people were killed in the house and one of the coppers said there wasn't a mark on their bodies. I get along with coppers when I have to. Not a mark on the bodies. And then, this morning, I get this call from Henry saying he's sending over his girl friend. Only he didn't call you his girl friend but I knew what you were. Take a look, Irish girl, take a look at this.''

Maureen stared at the bottle of vodka.

"Not vodka. He got this stuff special in Italy when we were staying there. He must have picked it up in Naples. It's not vodka. I can guess what it is after I saw the house in Mayfair and after the cop said all those people died without a mark. That's Henry, don't you get it, Maureen?''

"What are you saying?''

"Henry is setting up an act of terror for profit. He told you that, didn't he? He always tells a little bit of the truth to us girls, just to keep us interested.''

Maureen didn't notice she had lowered the knife. She opened the bottle of vodka and sniffed it.

"What is it?''

"Oh, I'm no chemist, I'm just a little rat girl who lives by her wits and Henry forgot that, forgot that I could steal for him and even kill for him if I had to but I wasn't a fool. Henry forgot I wasn't a fool.''

"So what is it?''

"I think it's a kind of gas. A poison gas. That's what killed those people in Trevor Armstrong's house in Mayfair.''

"Jesus,'' the Irish girl said. The knife was at her side. She understood the photographs of Matthew O'Day.

"Yes, Jesus and all the saints. I couldn't understand why we needed Irish terrorists to work for us but I can see it now. Matthew O'Day is the setup.''

The fall guy. It was exactly what Henry had said.

"And you, love, you're the other lamb for the slaughter."

"But you were—"

"No, lamb. We both were. Do you see this?"

"What is it?"

"A radio receiver. And this over here is something that looks like caviar but it smells like an explosive, a Plastique of some kind. So the radio receiver gets a signal—did Henry drive you here?"

"Yes."

"And didn't even bother to come in and see his old German girl and give her a peck or a quick fuck. I suppose you'd taken care of that for him. He likes it very rough sometimes and you'll have to get used to that."

"I'm not a whore," Maureen said.

"You fuck for money. What do you think that's called? Or do you have other names for it in Ireland?"

"I would have killed you—"

"And we'd both be dead anyway, love, if the radio receiver was still sitting in that Plastique. The Plastique would have somehow turned this liquid into gas and we'd be terminally dead. And when they found us, there'd be me and you and there'd be a link to Matthew O'Day and no link at all to Henry McGee. Did you really think he was going to take you off with him when he shakes down Trevor Armstrong?"

"Didn't you?"

"No. I thought he'd just leave me, though, not kill me. I should have thought it would have been enough for him." Now her voice was bitter and the rasp had returned to her words. The German gutturals cluttered the edges of the English words and made them even harder.

"He's made me angry, lamb. He thinks I'm so stupid."

"I was going to kill him," Maureen said. There was no threat from the knife anymore. Her eyes were empty. "He thought I was a whore but I was going to kill him. He convinced me Matthew betrayed us and I thought Matthew was in it from the first with Henry and it makes me mad to think I was so fookin' stupid. I was gonna kill him for the money. Take the money back to Ireland and use it the right way. Rebuild the network."

"You're a patriot, lamb. That's the most innocent thing of all."

"I was gonna even murder you for the money. And all the time he was humpin' me, he was figurin' I'd be dead in a couple of hours."

"It probably made it more exciting for him," Marie said. "Well—"

The telephone rang. The brisk burr of sound stilled both of them. Marie stared at Maureen. "It's Henry. He wants to make sure it worked."

"The bastard, I'll—"

Marie held up her hand.

She took a step toward Maureen. She smiled again, the grin made into a leer by the harsh kitchen lights.

"We'll," is all she said.

THIRTY-EIGHT

Hanley closed the door of conference room A. It was totally secure and could not even be bugged because of the silent electronic static emitted along the walls, floor, and ceiling. The room was painted white and had no windows. There was a single table of gun-metal gray with a Formica top and four metal chairs. Rita Macklin sat on one of the chairs with her hands folded on the table. She stared at Hanley and her eyes had pain in them.

"I don't know what this is about," Hanley began.

"Cut the lies, cut all the crap." The voice was stronger than the face would lead you to expect. She was frail and sick but not in her voice. "He called me from London and you know what this is about. He blanked out on me. It's the aftereffects of the drugs. He's not well and you sent him on a fucking mission. You are bastards, I've known what bastards you are, but not this time. Not when I almost have him back. Not now. I want you to find him and bring him back to me.''

''Miss Macklin, I can assure you—''

She shook her head. ''I can assure you, you bastard, that I'll hang you and hang goddamned Section this time. You can't booga-booga me and you can't get me.''

''Miss Macklin.'' Hanley sat down across from her. His eyes were mild and his words were soft. ''You've been under a strain. An understandable strain. You suffered a trauma. You were under neurological treatment as the result of your trauma.''

''And I'm crazy, right?'' she said.

''That's an unfortunate psychological term. Neurological—''

''Cut the crap, I told you that before.'' Her voice fell to a monotone. ''I want you to go after him and get him. If he goes against Henry McGee and forgets where he is or what he's doing, he'll be dead. If he's dead, you're dead. D-E-A-D. If he's dead, I go after you and R Section and your whole spook department, I go after it one by one and I tell everything I ever knew. I tell about the dirty jobs you gave him and the dirty jobs he did.''

''You would implicate yourself . . . in what you call 'dirty jobs.' You would put yourself beyond the pale of the law.''

She said, ''You don't seem to get it, Mr. Hanley. I don't care once he's dead. If he's dead, I'm dead, and then you can't hurt me. Not with threats or the law or whatever you call it. He's gone to sanction someone and that's illegal. I want you to act on this. Right now.''

It was four in the afternoon, four hours after Devereaux made his frightening call to Rita Macklin from Heathrow

Airport. It had taken that long to get to Hanley, but only a moment for her to decide what she would do. She had told Mac some of the things she was going to do, in case they stopped her or arrested her or locked her up in a sanitarium. Mac said he would do anything and she believed him.

"Oh, God, Mac," she had said. "I'm so afraid he's going to die this time. I really am."

And Mac had seen how much she had loved him. It had made him sad but he thought he could live with that.

Now Hanley drummed his fingertips on the Formica top of the table. This damned woman and her damned threats. She couldn't topple Section—Agee couldn't topple Langley when he spilled his guts—but she could hurt Section because she had been so close to things Devereaux had been involved in. This damned woman was a security problem from the beginning but Hanley had wished it away because there was no way Devereaux would have acquiesced to ending the relationship. And Devereaux had been a continuing problem.

"This is his last assignment," Hanley said.

"I've heard that before."

"We had begun the process of separation," Hanley said in the same mild voice. "A disability. He had been a problem for us for a while and this . . . trauma he suffered provided us with reasonable medical grounds to separate him from active duty. He knew this."

"He never told me," she said.

"He knew this. He also told us he wanted to get to Henry McGee. Henry McGee has been a continuing problem for us as well and his . . . mere existence threatens Section. I had certain information about the whereabouts of Henry McGee—"

"You sent him to London. He's in London. How close is he to Henry McGee?"

"Days. Hours. I don't know. I had no idea he had suffered . . . a mental incapacity—"

"It's Dr. Krueger, your goddamned Dr. Krueger."

"We're not in the medical business, Miss Macklin." A little ice was added to the voice. "Dr. Krueger was recommended to us. He was discreet and he had security clearance. He's in a mental ward right now, coming down from an overdose of lysergic acid. Apparently self-induced, but I think he must have had help along the way, don't you? And what was your part in it?"

Rita Macklin remembered the long scream from a darkened house and gripped her hands together. She looked at her hands and then at Hanley.

"Where was he booked for?"

"I don't understand—"

"I'm going to London. I'm not kidding you, Mr. Hanley, so don't think you can stall around. Where did Section book him?"

"We don't—"

"The fucking travel agency, Mr. Hanley. I don't have a lot of time, I've got to get to Dulles before seven. What hotel?"

Hanley gave in. "Hilton. It's in—"

"I know where it is. All right. If you can't help me, just remember I warned you." She got up. Hanley remained seated. She stared down at him. "Just remember, he better not die."

"Don't interfere in this. Let the matter be resolved—"

"And solve both your problems? Is that it? Getting rid of either of them helps you and your goddamned Section. Or getting rid of both of them? You are bastards, all of you, spooks and liars—"

Hanley waited for her to end but she interrupted herself.

A moment of silence passed between them.

"I mean it, Hanley. Just remember that. I really mean it."

"If you breach security, you can be prosecuted."

"Yes. And you can go to prison," she said and buttoned her coat. Her eyes were alive in their gaunt sockets. It was the rage in her. "You can go to hell, in fact, and I'll push you down the slide."

THIRTY-NINE

Henry McGee found Matthew O'Day at the bar in the little pub down the street from Paddington Station. It was just two in the afternoon and there had been so many things to do since meeting Trevor for lunch. He had left his salad but finished his whiskey. And left the bill for Trevor to pay.

"About time," Matthew said.

"You didn't enjoy the booze while you were waiting?"

The two men moved down the public room bar to the saloon side and entered. The saloon was carpeted while the public room was not. They ordered whiskeys and took them to a booth where the lights were dim.

"Well, then, what's it to be?" Matthew O'Day said. "And where the hell is Maureen?"

"Maureen is deader than Kelsey's nuts," Henry said.

Matthew froze. His hand covered the whiskey glass but it

was absolutely paralyzed. He stared at Henry and waited for another sound but none came for a long time.

"You killed her?"

"She was gonna kill you and I needed you a lot more than I needed her," Henry said. "She blamed you for the raid on the farm and for bombing the public house in the south and even for killin' little Brian Parnell. A murderous bitch, she had to be killed or she would have ruined everything. She was gonna off you tonight."

"I don't believe a fookin' word comin' out of your mouth," Matthew said.

"Listen to her yourself."

He had a microcassette Sony in his hand. He pushed the button. There was Maureen's voice, clear at times and cloudy at other times. "I'll kill Matthew for what he's done to us. Poor Brian. He killed Brian as sure as if he was standing in that urinal with him."

"I never killed Brian Parnell," Matthew said.

Henry chuckled and turned off the tape. "I know that and you know that but you couldn't convince her of it."

"She coulda killed me lots of times the last few days. Why tonight?"

"Because we're gonna make a move in three days and time was finally runnin' out," Henry said.

"Where is she?"

"Someplace safe. Nobody'll find her for days. Until she stinks too much and someone smells her rotting body."

"Jesus Christ, man. Ain't you got no nature to you? How'd you kill her?"

"The same way I killed the people in Mayfair. Nerve gas. Very humane. Attacks the central nervous system and you kind of do a fit. That's what I've been told. Sort of like epilepsy. A grand mal seizure. In any case, she's dead.''

"And the girl, the girl you sent to meet me in Dublin at the Horseshoe Bar—"

"My little Marie." Softly. "She's gone back to Berlin. She wants me to join her but she's got family there. Got a mother there, I understand; never met her." Henry grinned.

"What the hell is going on, man? Do you take me for a fool?"

"One hundred thousand pounds. British pounds. Trading at one point sixty-one in dollars. A nice bit of change. You did good on the first mission, now you'll finish it off and be on your way. I've booked you on a flight to Chicago at two P.M. Friday from Heathrow.''

"Why the hell would I want to go to fookin' Chicago?"

"To get out of here for a while, Matthew, and cool down. And to finish the thing off for me. Mr. Armstrong needs further convincing and so I'm gonna offer it to him. I've got an address for you in Chicago and another parcel to deliver when you get there. But this time, it really is a bomb, not a book.''

"What the hell is it that I want to do in Chicago?"

"I want you to blow up the ticket office of EAA. All you got to do is make another Federal Express delivery and walk away. And I know you're gonna do it, Matthew, because you wouldn't fail me now.''

"Why not do it yourself?"

"Because when the bomb goes off over there, I'm gonna be standing right next to Mr. Trevor Armstrong with a fucking metaphor pointed at his head and I'm gonna tell him that next time, EAA will have another plane fall out of the sky. An airline gets a bad reputation after a while. A long time ago, there was one of those once-in-a-million things where Air France had two crashes in one day. Well, they were devastated, especially when some television comedian started calling them 'Air Chance' and they had some rough years there. EAA had bad luck with terrorists once; they can have bad luck come in bunches if I can't shake the money tree.''

"So I'll be in Chicago and you're thousands of miles away and I trust you to take care of me, is that it? You must think I was born the day before yesterday. Do you take me for a fool?''

"No, sir, Matthew, I surely don't. I take you for an honest man.'' Henry paused, chuckled. "I'll give you a suitcase at Heathrow on Friday noon. You'll open it in the privacy of a stall in the men's room and you'll see it contains exactly what I said it would contain. Some shirts and shoes and junk like that. And seventy-five thousand pounds sterling Bank of England in God We Trust. Now you'll put the money in your pockets and you'll march over to the ticket counter and check your bag through and go into the lounge and wait to board. First class. And when you reach Chicago, get a hotel room, rest up—don't want you to suffer jet lag—and the next day, pick up a package at a certain address and take it to another address. You think you can follow that?''

"All right, what if I take the money and run? Did you think of that?''

"Did you think of who I am, Matthew? Did you think I could have started half the republic of Eire after your ass? Did you think I couldn't terrorize even the professionals? I'm the top of the league of terror, Matthew; I thought you'd realize that now. I'm the worst man in the world and if I didn't hear a bomb go off in Chicago, I'd just have to go after you. I learned to skin hides in Alaska years ago. I'm an Alaska man, did you know that? Can you imagine what it's gonna feel like when I find you and start peeling your skin off? Can you even imagine the pain of it? And when you pass out from the pain, I'll just wait till you come to again and we'll start again.''

The important thing was to make Matthew believe every word. Henry delivered the words very low and slowly and without any threat, just recitation of dull facts of life.

He saw that Matthew believed.

"Then I'm through with you. Once it's done?"

"Once it's done," Henry said. "I got tickets here. Another airline, not EAA. We don't want them spooked or looking for you. Another airline and you'll travel first class. You'll like it fine. Seven, eight hours and you get a good night's rest and then a simple delivery of a package. It's easy work, Matthew."

"Yes," Matthew said, seeing it from Henry's point of view.

And then he saw Maureen in his mind's eye lying dead somewhere, rotting.

He wiped his lips. He stared at the murderous man. "You take a share of pleasure in killin', I can see that."

"Good," Henry McGee said. "If you can see that, then you'll do the right thing for sure."

FORTY

Dwyer drove Trevor Armstrong home. Jameson and
Dennison were back at Oxford Circus not because Trevor
needed them to work late but because he needed to be alone
with Dwyer. Dwyer was his man, especially in this.

Night smothered London and the sky was orange with the
reflected lights from the city. The river Thames was black
but, here and there, sprinkled with gems of light from the
buildings along the Embankment. The new buildings beyond
Tower Bridge loomed up hideously in the night sky. The
modern architecture did not even try to blend into the graceful
Georgian landscape that had preserved an idea of the city for
two centuries. Trevor stared out the side window and began
to speak in a clear, distant voice to Dwyer, as though Dwyer
might be a disembodied spirit sent to converse with a disembodied Trevor.

"Where did he go?"

"To a public house in Paddington. I waited for him and even went into the public bar to spot who he was meeting. Looked like an Irish fellow, you know how they look. Wore a tweed coat and I caught the accent when he went to the bar for a whiskey. He drank Paddy."

"I know who it must be," Trevor said.

"Then he gave me the slip. Not that I think he spotted me but I think he was just doing something out of habit. The man I was following went back to the washrooms and never came out. After a while, the Irishman went back to his hotel. It's one of the little hotels down the street from Paddington Station."

"I want to get away from the police on Friday. I have to meet this same man at Heathrow. We'll be making an exchange."

"This isn't about Allison. Or the kid."

"No. This is about our survival, Dwyer."

The little man thought about it. The car swept along and everything about the night was crowded. London had a sense of cars, lorries, buses, and streets filled with people. It was a rare, warm November night and there was a gay spirit to the city that infected every stone and street.

"Dennison and Jameson aren't in on it."

"You and me, Dwyer."

"Like from the beginning, boss."

"Exactly."

"But what's it about?"

"I've been blackmailed."

Dwyer said nothing for a long time. Then: "I figured that."

"When did you figure it?"

"When I saw that book that was in the mail on the sideboard. It was the movie that was showing on One forty-seven when it went down. And when the cops came, you had thrown the envelope in the toilet and flushed it and the book was on the shelf in the library. I just figured two and two.''

"And you were smart enough to say nothing.''

"That's right, boss.''

"All right. A man wants me to give him a lot of money to leave EAA alone. I don't know if he had anything to do with the first bombing. But he certainly killed my household. I'm . . . in a bind, a financial bind. I owe a lot of money for a lot of stock purchases I've made. I can't afford to see EAA go through . . . any period of doubt. In six months, Dwyer, we'll be out of London and out of the airline business. And we'll be very, very rich.''

"You'll be rich.''

"I told you to buy EAA at forty-four.''

"I put everything in it.''

"Believe me, before this is over, it'll be bid at a hundred.''

"I believe you, boss,'' Dwyer said.

"What I have to do is, I have to give him the money. On Friday. At Heathrow. A lot of money in a suitcase.''

"All right,'' Dwyer said.

"Then I want you to get the money back for me,'' Trevor said. He did not look at the other man. "Do you think you can do that?''

"I can do that,'' Dwyer said.

"I mean, you can't terrorize him or threaten him or anything. That isn't what I mean,'' Trevor said.

"Don't worry, boss. I know just what you mean.''

Trevor sighed. For the first time that day, for the first time since it began, he felt at ease. Dwyer was loyal. Dwyer knew exactly what he meant for him to do.

FORTY-ONE

Hanley told Mrs. Neumann about it. When he was finished, she did not say anything for a long time. She went to the window in the corner office on the sixth floor of the Department of Agriculture Building where R Section was quartered, and looked down on Fourteenth Street all the way to the bridge. Night was coming to the capital. She had been chief of R Section for four years and they had taken a toll on her. The concerns of the world of intelligence had rounded her shoulders a little, and her eyes, while as sharp as ever, were etched with lines that had not been there before. Even her beloved husband, Leo, had noticed all the changes in her and accepted them with sadness.

"Devereaux was the last man to send after him," she said at last. "He was discharged from hospital a week ago. He's a sick man."

247

"There's no time. If we can't get Henry back, he'll fall into the wrong hands."

"We've had our hands on him before." She turned from the window to look at him. "Miss Macklin will do all the things she threatened."

Hanley said, "Yes."

"You haven't really told me everything."

"I've told you everything."

"But not the part where Devereaux is going to kill Henry McGee." Her voice was gruff as always, a smoker's voice from one who had never smoked. "He's going to kill Henry, isn't he?"

"We do not sanction people."

"I know. I know your games, Hanley."

"I did not authorize any sanction."

"This is a wet contract and you've put him up to it because he wants to do it. He said he had been hit by Henry and we didn't believe him at first. And now we're afraid he was right and he gets our authority to . . . do what? Make an arrest? Call the British in, let them arrest him and turn him over to us."

"No," Hanley said. "It can't be handled that way."

"It's the right way to do this," she said.

"Mrs. Neumann, it is not the right way but I give you your choices. I will resign immediately from Operations. If your character cannot see the right thing to do, even if it's the wrong thing in some ways, then I won't be a part of the destruction of Section. I was here from the beginning. Henry knows too much now, about the deal in Europe last year in the case of that translator. We let Henry go a second time and we hoped the Russians would finish him off for us. You know that and you knew it then. But the Russians have other fish to fry for the time being and they won't do our wet work for us and we're stuck with the fact of Henry McGee. Yes, I think Devereaux will kill him and that will end the matter for us. Except for the complication now of Miss Macklin. In the event he does not kill Henry. What do we do about Miss Macklin?"

"She's an American citizen."

"Yes."

"There's not much we can do. She's a journalist."

"We can do an S job," Hanley said. He was very calm. They had never spoken of such things to each other.

"That would only be partly effective."

"Slander, Mrs. Neumann. It doesn't kill anyone. We'll put the FBI on her and follow her publicly and let it leak that she is a spy and has always been a spy and that she sold secrets to the Russians at the embassy in Mexico. She was there in March and she did go to the embassy. We even have a photograph of her entering the embassy from our permanent watcher. She went to the embassy for an interview but that's neither here nor there. We can follow her. We can investigate her. And we can ruin her. It's been done before."

"The hounds of hell. Follow her and slander her and let the slander build its own case against her."

"Yes. We can limit damage if we have to."

Mrs. Neumann put her thumb and index finger over the bridge of her nose and covered her eyes while she squinted. She might have been in pain. Hanley understood the pain.

"If we have to, S," Mrs. Neumann said. "We can also support Devereaux, can't we?"

"No. Whatever is happening is happening now and it is very close to being over and I don't know how we can send in support at this late date. I have an open line to London

Station but he hasn't made contact. You know how he works in black. He's not going to make contact because he doesn't want to involve anyone else. I don't even know exactly where Devereaux is at this moment—''

"Hanley. This was the wrong thing."

Hanley nodded. "But it was necessary because this was the time for wrong things."

FORTY-TWO

Trevor Armstrong stood before the fireplace and stoked the oaks that Dwyer had ignited. It was a damned nuisance not to have staff at the moment. Dwyer had to be general factotum.

A glass of whiskey rested on a marble coaster on the sideboard. He went to it, picked it up, and tasted the Laphroiag.

Dwyer had disappeared up the stairs for his bedroom at the back of the house where he had his telly and VCR and his own stock of whiskey. Sometimes he had a girl there but only on nights when the staff and the boss were gone.

"Please don't make a sound, Mr. Armstrong," Devereaux said.

He stepped into the room from the entry hall. He held a pistol in his right hand. The pistol and all the other things he needed had been waiting for him at the Hilton Hotel when he arrived. They were packaged by the safe house in Fleet Street and included the standard pharmacopoeia as well as items of trickery like lighters filled with gas. And a pistol, a standard 9mm Beretta.

"Who are you? How did you get in here?"

"You brought me in. I was in the trunk. Or boot. You and your friend drove into the garage and past the police guards."

"Who are you?"

"Sit down."

Trevor thought to make reply for a moment and then thought better of it. He chose the leather wing chair closest to the fire. He sat down and waited, his hands joined in a casual gesture, his head tilted toward the man with the gun.

The gunman sat on the hearth bricks, his back to the crackling flames. He stared at Trevor's face for a moment, studying it. Then he reached in his inside jacket pocket and removed a photograph. He handed the picture to Trevor.

Trevor studied the front view and profile of Henry McGee. The picture was the last taken of him, three years earlier, when he had been arrested for espionage.

Trevor held the photograph for the proper length of time and then handed it back to the man with the gun.

Devereaux said, "I know you've seen him."

"I don't know what you're talking about."

"I want to know what he wants from you."

"I've never seen that man before."

Devereaux studied the lie. He was certain it was a lie and he wondered why. People lie out of terror sometimes, but terror replaces terror and he was the man with the gun at the moment. That should have been enough.

"What does he want from you? What's the threat?"

"I don't know who you are or what you want," Trevor said. "This house has police around it, as you know. How do you propose to get out of here? I think you should be concerned with that more than anything else."

"I didn't expect you to lie," Devereaux said. It was the truth. Something here went beyond the fact of Henry McGee and the fact that Henry was a terrorist.

He wasn't prepared to do anything about it. There were police outside. He had hidden in the car to get close to Trevor, to see him alone, to let him know he had a gun and had managed to penetrate the security around the house. But what could he do now?

"Henry McGee is his name," Devereaux said. "Did you know that? He's wanted by the United States government. He broke out of prison nearly two years ago. He's wanted for espionage against the government. He's a terrorist and a killer."

"And who are you?"

"My name is Devereaux. I'm a field intelligence agent for R Section."

"I never heard of it."

"It doesn't matter. It exists. I'm sorry I didn't have business cards printed up."

"Even if I believe you, I can't help you. I mean, I never saw that man before in my life." It was easier now; the other man had a name, shape, form, and purpose. He was nothing but a cop of some sort.

"Tell me why you deny you know Henry." Quietly.

The sound of full Westminster echoed into the dark room. Sixteen notes in solemn procession followed by the tolling of the chimes. Nine chimes for the hours.

Devereaux said, "You should tell me."

"I don't know what you're talking about. I'm a citizen of the United States."

"I know. The government appreciates your cooperation."

"The government has no right to break into my house and violate my privacy. Will you put that pistol away?"

Devereaux did. He still waited and stared at the other man. Trevor said, "If I had any information, I'd help you."

"Four people were killed in this house. Why do you suppose it would matter to Henry if you were one more? You can't deal with terrorism the way you want to deal with it."

"I don't know anything about 'terrorism,' as you put it."

"Except for Flight One forty-seven."

"The authorities are investigating that. The British have narrowed the circle of suspects. You must know all this. What did you call this fellow? Henry McGee? Is he one of the suspects? I don't recall that name or that face."

"Will Henry blow up one of your aircraft if you don't pay him? How much does he want?"

It was very close and it began to worry Trevor. The worry began to show in the eyes because the pupils moved back and forth, trying to find focus either on the man in the shadows or in the flames behind him.

"How much does he want?" Devereaux said again.

"I really don't think I can help you," Trevor said. "I'm sorry. Obviously something—some person or persons—has attempted some sort of terrorism here in my home but I don't honestly know for what purpose. It's the reason the police are following me everywhere—"

"Yes. Everywhere," Devereaux said. He decided then and sighed. He stood up. "Good night, Mr. Armstrong."

"You needn't have hidden yourself in my automobile to see me. I'm in the offices every day. My door is open."

"Yes," Devereaux said. "Perhaps I'll come around and show this photograph to your staff. Perhaps they've seen this man."

Devereaux stood very close to Trevor and saw the effect of his words.

"Well, we can arrange something, I suppose," Trevor said. "I don't like my staff bothered by the police. They have nothing to do with this."

"But what is this, Trevor?"

"I don't understand."

"What is this really about, Trevor?"

"You break into my house and put rude questions to me. By what authority, Mr. Devereaux?"

Devereaux waited a moment longer to let him at least feel the intimidation in his presence. And then he turned.

"How will you get out of here?"

"With your permission," Devereaux said. "Whatever it is you're doing, Trevor, you don't want to draw the attention of the London police to yourself. In case I am who I say I am."

"And if you are an . . . agent of this . . . whatever it is, a legitimate representative of the United States, why aren't you cooperating with the police in the first place? Hiding in the trunk of my car like that?"

Devereaux smiled. His smile lighted the wan, gray face in a strange way that unnerved Trevor. He felt the beginning of a tremor in his left hand, the one that held his drink.

"Yes. That's the problem. We make decisions all the time. I'll leave by the front door and it'll be your decision, whether to call the police guard on me. And on yourself. Good night, Trevor."

He walked to the front entry hall and opened the front door.

The policeman on the sidewalk turned to look at him and at Trevor standing behind him in the door.

"Good night, Trevor," Devereaux said. He started down the three steps to the walkway. He turned again, standing in front of the policeman, and said, "I'll see you soon."

Trevor said, "Yes."

Devereaux said to the policeman, "Good evening."

"Good evening, sir," the policeman said.

And Devereaux knew then that Trevor Armstrong was going to complicate the matter of getting Henry McGee.

FORTY-THREE

M aureen pushed the barrel against his ear. The street-lamp was out because she had seen to that. They were scarcely a hundred feet from Trevor's front door and she could see the policeman there, although he could not see her.

"Good evenin', fella, and don't say a word in reply or you'll lose your hearing and a few other faculties."

Devereaux stood still.

"Walk round the corner with me, love, and don't even think of running away."

Devereaux walked around the corner and they were out of sight of the town house. A blue Ford Escort sat on the curb in a yellow-striped no-parking zone. A ticket was affixed to the windshield wiper.

"Open the boot, fella," she said in her throaty voice.

"You could have picked a bigger car," Devereaux said.

"I told you about talkin'." She slapped the side of his head with the pistol barrel and he crumpled half into the trunk. She put the pistol in her raincoat and picked up his legs and crammed him into the rest of the trunk. She closed the lid.

Maureen drove out to Maida Vale and then down the Edgware Road to the street where Marie Dreiser waited for her. It was part one of the plan, to get the money and to get Henry McGee at the same time, and it had worked so smoothly that Maureen was sure the rest would work as well. Henry had been right about one thing: you couldn't go on with a person like Marie, she was crazy as a bedbug, and once they had fixed matters with Trevor Armstrong and with Henry, there'd be no splitting of the five million. Five million cash and she'd have no trouble financing the revolution and finding the volunteers. Only this time, they'd follow her plans and her way of thinking. There was only one enemy and the way to get that enemy was to target them, not pub crawlers in Belfast. Kill the English bastards and start at the top with the governors of the state, the ministers and toadies and MPs who voted the wrong way consistently on the question of Ulster. Oh, she had some big ideas all right and Marie wouldn't figure in them so she'd have to be a victim. And what did it matter anyway? She was just a terrorist-for-profit, corrupting Matthew O'Day in his greed to betray the farm and the cause.

By the time she reached the flat, she had justified herself to herself completely.

The street was dark, gloomier than the average residential block in London because of the excess of trees and the absence of streetlamps, all knocked out by Maureen.

She opened the trunk and held the pistol against his head. He was awake.

"D'ya see, fella, the way it is?"

"I see."

"Then crawl out careful like and we'll go inside."

They went up the steps to the door. "Ring the bell," Maureen said, putting the prod of the revolver in his back.

He rang the bell.

Marie opened the door. She stared at him.

Maureen grinned viciously. "Mister Trevor Armstrong, at your service," she said.

Devereaux looked at the girl he had known in Rome more than a year before. The woman whose life he had saved. She stared back at him.

"Well, ain't ya gonna say nothin'?"

Devereaux's cheek was bruised. His eyes were terrible and gray and sick.

"What should I say?" Marie said. "You got the wrong man, Maureen. You stupid bitch, you got the wrong man."

Maureen's face fell.

Devereaux stood between the two women.

"He come out of that house, he talked to the copper on the walk, he—"

"He's the wrong man. He isn't Trevor Armstrong," she said.

"Then who the hell is he then?" She prodded him with the pistol and reached into his pocket. She found the automatic.

"A fookin' gun? He's from the fookin' police then? I picked me up a fookin' copper," Maureen said. The smile began again and it wasn't very nice. "A fookin' pig, love, I got me a pig to make squeal—"

"Be quiet, Maureen, are you crazy, you want to fire that thing in here?"

"Then I'll cut his throat—"

"And we'll walk around a corpse for the next week? Get rid of him someplace else, I don't care."

Devereaux looked at her. Her eyes were tough. What did she owe him? Another fucking policeman, the world had too many to start with. What had he done for her?

But save her life.

"I don't owe you anything," she said to him.

Maureen pulled back the gun. "You know him? You know this copper?"

"He's no copper," Marie said. "I knew him in Berlin. *Ein volk*, eh?"

"*Ein volk*," Devereaux said.

"What the hell does that mean?"

"He was in the American consulate there. He picked me up and gave me candy, didn't you, lamb? We were all the same, eh? *Ein volk*."

"Yes," Devereaux said.

"Then he's a fookin' American diplomat? Is that it?"

"That's it," Marie said.

"And he's carrying a pistol?"

"He carried a pistol in Berlin. I suppose it's the same here, eh? You never know when you're going to be kidnapped." And Marie laughed. "You never know where and when and by whom. Us, lamb, it was a couple of girls that did it."

"The point is, what do you do now?"

"Why were ya talkin' with Armstrong?"

"That's obvious, isn't it? The matter of Flight One forty-seven. The plane that went down."

"Jesus," Maureen said. She had fucked up. "Jesus," was all she could think to say.

"Oh, no," Marie said. "Maybe we can turn this thing around for us."

Maureen said, "We're gonna have to off him, no matter what."

"Yes," Marie said. "No matter what. But if we off him right away, we'll screw up the rest of the plan. The city will be crawling with coppers, SAS men, army people; they'll stop everyone and especially foreigners. That's you, love, and me. So let's not do this thing right away."

"So what do we do?"

"Tie him up first and decide later about it. We got things to do first," Marie said. She was staring at Devereaux and smiling at him in a mean way. "Would you like a little bondage, mister? I remember you liked bondage in Berlin. You liked to tie me up and spank me; would you like it the other way around?"

"I'd never let a man do that to me," Maureen said.

"Oh," Marie said, coming out of a reverie of events that never happened. "It's not so bad. It's not the worst thing. When you get hungry enough, nothing is that bad anymore."

Devereaux said nothing. This was all Marie's game, her fantasy and her show. She had just saved his life but not promised not to take it in the long run. Was she just giving him a little time or was she giving herself time to decide something?

"Get down the hall, lamb," Marie said. She had one pistol, the one taken from him, and Maureen had the other. The women were dressed alike, in black and without makeup, and their faces were cold and murderous. They might have been sisters.

They made him strip to his underwear. There was kitchen clothesline and Marie cut it into pieces just long enough to tie his wrists to the headboards and his feet to the footboard. And then she wrapped a scarf around his eyes and around his mouth.

Marie sat down on the bed next to him then. She ran her hand on his chest. She had seen the scars of the operations, still healing and angry.

"Let me alone with him, I want to play with him," she said to Maureen.

The other woman left the room and closed the door.

Marie came very close to his ear. "Who hurt you, lamb? You're all scars. They hurt you bad, didn't they, whoever it was?"

She took the gag out of his mouth.

She waited.

"Henry," he said.

"Why did you come here?"

"To kill him."

"You didn't kill him before. Why now?"

"Because I had no reason."

"Why do you have a reason now, lamb?" And she stroked his naked chest with her hand in a soft, sensuous way.

"Where is he, Marie?"

"The other one knows. We don't trust each other too much so we're waiting on each other. On Henry's game."

"What's the game, Marie?"

"What's it always, love? It's money." And she kissed him, a long and lingering kiss, and he received it and returned it. And when she was finished, she pulled her head back and laughed in a low voice. "Do you want to seduce me, lamb? Make me untie you?"

"Untie me," he said.

"I can't do that, lamb. I owe Henry McGee too much to let you get him. The other one. She's insane, you know, a patriot. An Irish patriot. She wants to get the money to save Ireland from England. If that isn't insane, tell me what is."

"What's the money, Marie? Is it from Trevor? What's it for, Marie?"

"To stop the terror, love," she said, stroking his chest again. She traced the line of a scar. "Henry did all this to you? How did he do it?"

"A bomb," Devereaux said.

"He killed those people in Trevor's house. You knew that."

"I guessed that."

"But does everyone else know?"

"No."

"Who sent you, Devereaux?"

"I sent myself," Devereaux said.

"A pure matter of revenge. Well, don't worry, love. I'll take care of Henry McGee and he won't get away and there won't be any second thoughts from me. Henry is dead and that crazy girl out there is going to be dead and I'm going to live. The only problem is you, Devereaux. You did save my life and that was important to me. Maybe not then but it is now. Now that Henry wants to take it. He could have left my life, I didn't expect anything out of the bastard but he could have left me a shred of life. So much the worse for him."

"And what about me, Marie?"

"That's the problem. If I save your life this time, you'll turn on me when you get the chance. You're just a policeman underneath everything and policemen are scum and they are the enemy all the time.''

''I won't turn on you.''

She kissed him again, very hungry and wet, and he let himself be kissed. And when she pulled back, her eyes were wild. ''You won't huh? You promise, lamb? You truly promise? Will you take an oath on it? I'm sorry I don't have a Bible with me but then, this isn't a hotel room. If we were lying together in a hotel room all naked and sweating, I could go and get a Bible out of the dresser and have you make an oath while you're screwing me.''

She laughed at him then. He couldn't see her but he felt her weight shift on the bed and then she was off the mattress and she wasn't touching him anymore. ''I'll think about it, lamb, while I'm doing what has to be done. I'll think about killing you or not killing you. I really will. But I think I know what I'm going to do and I want to apologize for it now because you did save my life. But that's the way it is, love. That's just the way of the rotten fucking world.''

FORTY-FOUR

"Good morning, Mr. Armstrong. Cassidy here." The absolutely terrible British accent was back with the familiar voice and Armstrong was waiting for it this time. It was Thursday morning. He had assembled four of the five million dollars and Dwyer was in Zurich at this very moment making the final withdrawal. But Trevor felt more in control than he had before.

"Good morning, Henry McGee. You can drop the accent."

A long silence followed and Trevor smiled. He was alone in his big office on the sixth floor off Oxford Circus.

"Who gave you the name?"

"A man named Devereaux. Do you know a man by that name?"

Another long silence.

When Henry spoke again, his voice was careful. "It can't be," Henry said.

"He said that was his name. He was from some section with the letter of the alphabet as a name. I don't believe in that but I do believe you're a wanted criminal. A known felon, as it were. At least, he showed me your arrest photograph."

"Devereaux is dead."

"He didn't look well but I can assure you he wasn't dead."

"Describe him."

He did.

Yet another pause. This time Trevor broke the silence: "Are you there, Henry? Hope I haven't given you too much of a shock."

"Nothing shocks me," Henry said in his old voice. "So Devereaux's here. That don't change nothing. You got the money?"

"I got the money. You got the other thing?"

"Matthew will be on the plane at two P.M. I thought we might watch him from the departure lounge."

"That's agreeable. How are you going to do it?"

"The bomb? That was simple. He gets a suitcase and he gets his money in it. He goes into the little boys' room and opens the case. That arms the bomb. He takes out the money and closes the case. That triggers the bomb on a six-hour fuse. He checks in his baggage, goes to the departure gate, gets aboard. The plane takes off. The trigger and timer are in the brass locks on top of the case and the explosive is in the lining. Fuckin' brilliant, don't you think?"

"And he suspects nothing?"

"He suspects everything, so what? He'll see his cut in front and cream."

"How much is it?"

"A hundred grand total, counting the first payout."

"My God, you're going to blow up a hundred thousand dollars?"

"Pounds. And yes, I am. You gotta spend money to make money. It's the way to get Matthew on the plane. And by the time it goes off, you'll be back at the office and I'll be someplace where you can't get second thoughts about me."

"Who is Devereaux?"

"A man who should be dead. He's nothing to you, Trevor."

"He fucking came to me, Henry. He knows I've seen you. He's after you."

"I know that. I knew that the minute you said his name. The point is, he can't get me."

"Is that true? Should I put this thing on hold? Should I go to the authorities instead?"

"Listen, Trevor, there's nothing you can do now. You got your stock at eighty today and Carl Greengold is making his move in New York. All you got to do is hold on for a few days, a week, and you got enough to bail out, pay your creditors and have enough to retire on. You could afford to pay taxes with the money you're going to make out of this."

Trevor nodded into the receiver.

"Trevor."

"Yes."

"Believe me."

"I believe you."

"Or believe this. If you get chickenshit on me, I'll do to you what I told Matthew I would do to him."

"I'm tired of threats."

"I'm tired of making them. Especially when people don't believe me the first time. Still believe in me, Trevor?"

"Yes," Trevor Armstrong said.

"Good. Then don't sweat Devereaux. He can't do anything to you because he can't do anything to me. And thanks for the warning, Trevor. I owe you one."

FORTY-FIVE

Devereaux worked at the clothesline binding his left hand. It had seemed the most promising when he started.

That had been two hours ago.

The flat was silent. They were gone or sleeping.

The line had rubbed his wrist raw and each act of trying to slip the bond was accompanied by pain. But he thought it was working. It was difficult to tell because he couldn't see his hand.

He strained and then relaxed; strained; relaxed. The principle was that all cloth ropes and strings have play in them if you can work at the play and have the time and patience. Each time he felt the line edge higher to the ridge formed by the back of his hand.

And then he was free, just like that.

He snatched the blindfold away and reached for the line

binding his right hand. He managed to untie the simple knot and then sat up on the bed and reached for the ropes on his legs.

He crept out of bed and slipped into his clothes, which lay on the floor.

The next part was harder. Two murderous women with guns were in the house.

He went into the hallway. The flat was perfectly still in the darkness. He stepped on a floorboard and it creaked. He went down the hallway to the kitchen.

Sullen moonlight filled the room and made shadows on the white walls.

He went to the back door and studied the locks. There were two of them, one a deadbolt. He carefully turned the locks and they clicked and he thought the noise was too loud.

He heard a sound from another part of the flat. He opened a drawer and took out a knife. He went back to the kitchen entry and waited, his back pressed against the kitchen wall.

In a moment, he saw Maureen in the moonlight. She was naked, except for the pistol in her hand. She pushed open the door of the room where he had been tied up.

"Shit," she said. "Fookin' gone, he is."

She passed down the hall toward the kitchen and Devereaux jumped her as she entered it. He grabbed her from behind, one hand on her right arm pushing the pistol forward, the other drawing the knife against her throat.

Maureen turned to struggle and the razor edge cut a line of blood across her throat.

"Don't," he said.

She stopped struggling. She held the pistol still but her aim and control were immobilized by Devereaux's hand.

"Drop the pistol."

"Then you'll kill me—"

"Drop the pistol."

She dropped the pistol, which clattered on the kitchen tiles. In that moment, Devereaux kicked her away from him and knelt to retrieve the gun. She came back at him with a snarl but now he had the gun.

"We shoulda killed ya, ya bastard."

"Where is she?"

"Right here, love, right behind you."

He turned and Marie had a pistol aimed at his chest. She was wearing a sleeping gown of white cotton that was too large for her. Her hair was tousled. Her eyes were very bright in the moonlight.

He held his pistol steady and looked at her. Maureen stood less than six feet away, her hands away from her body as though she were about to leap.

"I'll shoot you," Devereaux said in a calm, detached voice.

"Oh, yes, lamb, I believe that. I believe you'd never hold a gun unless you intended to use it. But it doesn't matter what you intend. The gun isn't loaded."

The pistol was an automatic and there was no way to tell if Marie was lying or not. He stared at her. The gamine turned to Maureen and smiled. "You see, love, I don't trust you either."

"You fookin' bitch, you and him are in something together—"

"I'm in everything for me, alone for me. I sent you to fetch Trevor Armstrong and you bring me back the wrong man. Should I trust you to do the right thing next time, dear?

But maybe you'd think to do the wrong thing the next time. Why should I trust you, any more than Matthew O'Day should trust you?''

Maureen saw the way it was. Her tone changed. She took a step toward Marie. She held out her hand. ''Look, you and I want the same thing.''

Marie turned the pistol toward Maureen. ''Do we? What do you want, Maureen? You want the money for yourself, don't you?''

Devereaux did not make a move. The two women had the scene.

''Come on. If the pistol's not loaded, then off the fuckin' pig. Do it now.''

Marie stared at Maureen.

''You're absolutely right. There's no point in waiting any longer.''

Maureen smiled at Devereaux.

Marie raised the pistol.

Devereaux pulled the trigger.

They all heard the sharp, short click of a hammer coming down on an empty chamber.

Marie fired once.

The bullet caught Maureen between her breasts and drove her backward, off her feet. Her eyes were simply amazed and they remained wide open after the moment of death. Her head struck the kitchen table but she didn't feel a thing. She fell onto the floor.

Devereaux stood still.

Marie turned to him. A little smoke came from the barrel. She said, ''Henry wanted to kill me. He didn't have to do that.''

''He wanted to kill me.''

"Yes. Henry likes bombs. I've come to learn that. He wanted to kill me and her and now I've done it to her because there was no other way. You see that?"

Devereaux said nothing.

"You have to see that," Marie said.

"If you say so."

"She was a terrorist. She would have killed you when she brought you back. I saved your life then, lamb."

"I know."

"And what should I do with it now?"

Devereaux waited.

"I could kill you. Oh, yes, I'm not afraid to do that. But then it would remind me that you saved my life. I should show how grateful I am. Would you like me? Would you like me to do things for you? I can do anything, you know." Marie smiled.

"Including murder. How are you going to kill Henry?" Devereaux said.

"The quickest way I can. And get the money he's cheating out of Trevor Armstrong."

"I don't care about the money. I want to get Henry McGee," Devereaux said.

"Because of what he did to you."

"Because of what he did to a woman."

Marie caught her breath in surprise. Then she smiled. "What did he do to a woman? Some woman you liked?"

"He shot her."

"Is she dead?"

"No."

"Then you got a girl, lamb? Could you spare a little of yourself for me?"

"I want Henry McGee."

"What do you want to do with him?"

"I think I know now," Devereaux said. He still held the empty pistol and he was staring straight into her mad eyes.

And it was enough.

She took a step back and slowly folded her arms across her chest and still held the pistol but not pointed at him. She leaned against the wall and cocked her head and they stared at each other for a long moment.

Then she said, smiling, "Tell me."

FORTY-SIX

W hy was this so easy?

It was the only question that still bothered Henry McGee as he took the elevator to the sixth floor of the Hilton Hotel in west central London.

In his right pocket was a pistol but he didn't expect to use the Walther. In the left jacket pocket were the makings of a bomb.

Second time lucky, he thought. And he smiled at the thought while facing a drab American man with travel-tired eyes and bags in his hands and under his eyes. The man did not understand the smile and did not respond to it; his mind had been dulled by days of business and incessant travel to the point where every hotel was the same, every airport was really one big airport, and the taste of food was even gone.

Henry would never feel such tiredness. He had traveled

everywhere in the world, eaten every food, slept with every kind of woman, pretended to be on one side and then the other, and the zest of living every moment was enough to keep his eyes shining, even during the deliberate grind of the nearly two years he had been forced to spend in prison. In prison. Because of that bastard, Devereaux. That was why he came back and would come back and back and back until Devereaux was meat for dogs.

Devereaux had registered here under the name of Dever. That was easy enough to get out of the store of memory in London Station. The trouble with R Section was that it was so fucking penetrable, especially by a former agent turned traitor named Henry McGee.

The Hilton would be right. It was the kind of place—big, anonymous, American to the core—where Section would put its agents on missions abroad. The mission was fairly obvious. To get Henry McGee. A wet contract of the sort that the United States was never supposed to put out.

Henry smiled at that thought too. He stepped off the elevator at the sixth floor, leaving the tired salesman still in the cage. He went down the hallway to the door of the room.

It was almost too easy, he thought. So he also thought it might be some kind of a setup.

He knocked at the door and waited. He had not expected an answer.

A long moment passed. He used a thin piece of steel shaped like a credit card with various edges cut out of it to pull open the lock. The card was his own invention, something he had learned to make in the prison machine shop. It opened bottles, cans, and doors. Clever old Henry; he'd have to get a patent for it someday if he ever needed money again. Call it the Real McGee, tell people don't leave home without it.

The room contained a suitcase on a sideboard. The case was open. Henry went through it with considerable efficiency. The second case was on a writing desk. He recognized it for what it was; hadn't he used such cases when he was in Section, let alone when he was traveling for KGB? It was the case of a killer on a mission that was deniable from the beginning.

"Fuckin' R Section," he muttered. He touched the extra rounds banded in automatic clips. They had exploding tips that blew apart the hollow aluminum on contact and shredded into the body of the person contacted. Tips for murder most extreme, no matter where they hit you.

Henry realized he was working himself up. He didn't care. He enjoyed it the way he enjoyed everything, even killing Maureen and Marie with that gas device in the flat.

He took the makings of a bomb out of his left pocket. The bomb was simple Plastique. You could form it in your hand like clay. It was malleable and patient.

The second part of the bomb was the wire that led to the triggering device. The triggering device was actually plastic and aluminum. Once the parts were together, the device was armed. When Devereaux opened the door of the room, he would pull the trigger on his own bomb and send himself to his own death. It had not worked in that room in Washington but Henry McGee didn't have time to fool around with Devereaux, time to stalk him and shoot him down. This was going to have to do. It would do. Even a cat runs out of lives; Devereaux wouldn't survive again.

And the beauty part was that Devereaux wouldn't expect it again. Not twice. Not from the same man.

Henry McGee began to hum as he worked in the half darkness of the anonymous hotel room. Great London was mute beyond the double-paned windows and the throb of traffic stilled.

Arming the trigger was like operating a money clip that has a spring to hold the money against the metal side. Once the spring is pushed down, the tension holds the paper currency tight; and once the spring is released, the money slips away.

He was humming "Amazing Grace," he realized. What dim time in memory of childhood had the song been retrieved from? The Methodist church in the village in the bleak Alaskan tundra where he was raised?

> *". . . that saved a wretch like me?*
> *I once was lost, but now I'm found,*
> *Was blind but now I see . . ."*

There. It was finished. He got up from the chair and went to the door.

He paused at the knock.

Who the hell was knocking at the door? Devereaux wasn't knocking at the door of his own room. The bed was made, it was late morning, it couldn't be the maid again.

He listened to the knock again. And then he heard the voice.

"Dev."

Jesus Christ. He smiled. A fucking girl. Devereaux was nearly as much of a cocksman as he was.

He went to the door and opened it.

It was her.

The girl in the parking lot. The girl friend. Rita Macklin. They both fucking didn't die. He had killed them both and they both didn't die.

She just stared at him because she had never seen him before but she knew—knew right to her heart—exactly who he was. She was before the beast and it took her breath away for a moment and then she realized the beast could move.

He reached for her arm just as she had decided to turn and run down the hall.

He pulled her into the room and slammed the door with his foot. She started to scream and he slapped her very hard across the face and the blow stunned her to silence. He pushed her down on the bed and knelt over her and grinned down at her.

"You got more than one life too, huh, honey? You know I was the one shot you. You went down easy enough, you must be a late kill, huh? You and Devereaux. What's Devereaux's girlfriend look like under those clothes?"

He had knelt on her arms and all she could do was shake her head back and forth in struggle. Henry grinned at her helplessness and then he thought about it. He really didn't know how much time he had and the girl was a complication.

Damn, he nearly said aloud.

Slowly, he crawled off her. He could use the sheets, he decided, and pulled a knife out of his pocket. She gasped and thought it was meant for her.

Henry smiled. "No, honey, I ain't got time for folderol today. After tomorrow, I'll have plenty of time and money but you won't be around after tomorrow. So why don't we just end it here, what do you say?"

"What the hell are you talking about?"

He grabbed the top sheet and started a tear with the knife. She was dressed for travel—jeans, sweater, flat jogging shoes—and she started to get up from the bed.

"Nah," he said. "Get back in on your back and spread out your arms, honey. There. There and there."

The bonds were brutally tight. When he had finished trussing her to the bed, she began to feel her hands grow numb.

"They're too tight," she started to say.

"So your hands and feet are going to get numb. You think this is some sex game? You're tied down to stay down until your lover man comes to get you. And you won't like this gag either."

When he was finished, Henry said, "Now, see the way it is, you and loverboy are going to get killed together. Isn't that romantic? You and him going off to eternity, hand in hand. Sort of." He was working on the bomb again on the front door, positioning the triggering device in the jamb. He opened the door after applying the Plastique to the doorframe at eye level.

"Now, honey, adieu. When your friend comes tripping down the hall to find the love of his life in his bed, he's gonna have about a quarter of a second to appreciate the gift I wrapped for him before you and him are history. Understand what I'm saying, honey? This is a bomb and this time, it's gonna take both of you out. I like bombs, always have, always like to use them for the delayed effect. I know I won't be there when it goes but I can read all about it in the papers next day. Read all about the grievin' widows and perplexed police and all the rest of that good shit. So, so long, honey, you got time to think about it while you wait for him. Too bad I ain't got time to give you a good one but that's the way it goes." And he blew her a kiss at the door and slowly closed it on the triggering device.

FORTY-SEVEN

F riday.

Matthew O'Day was standing at a magazine counter staring at the cover of *Time* magazine. It was a shot of the ruined public house in County Clare where nineteen had died in Henry McGee's act of terror and the headline said: Why Ireland Still Weeps.

He glanced at the English papers arrayed on a counter beneath the magazine rack. The headlines were all about a bomb blast the day before in the Hilton Hotel. The world was full of bombs and sudden, certain acts of death and it was becoming just too much to understand and even know. Terror was beginning to seep into the fabric of society so deeply that acts of terror—like acts of murder or suicide or drug use—were numbing the public sensibility. Terror was beginning not to terrorize. Matthew O'Day was beginning to see that and see that there would have to be another way for him. Perhaps, when he came back from Chicago, he would recruit a force of assassins who would change the face of terror more along the lines suggested by this crazy American. Terror for profit and then assassination for political purpose. He thought of the botched bombing of the British government a decade earlier. You had to be sure and certain and nothing was more sure and certain than a bullet in the head. That was terror that made sense.

He looked around him at the hordes shuffling through the noise-filled terminal to gates and waiting planes. The world did not stop because a plane fell out of the sky. The government did not fall because a bomb made life just that little bit more untenable in Belfast. Matthew saw the way it was and saw the only way to go now was to make sense out of terror.

"I got your bag," Henry McGee said. It was a plain brown suitcase with brass-fitted locks. "And your tickets."

"I'll use me Eire passport in the name of Powers," Matthew said. "You've got the money now, and no tricks?"

"The money and no tricks. I want you to contact this number when you're in Chicago," Henry said, handing him a piece of paper.

Matthew looked warily at him and at the suitcase. "Like you said, I'll check it out meself," Matthew said.

"Like I said. Check it out and I'll wait until you go through ticketing. I'll be watching you, Matthew, so don't think you're going to do a duck on me with this money. You fuck me up and it's strip steak time, only you're the stripped steak."

Matthew took the bag into the men's room at the far end of the magazine kiosk. Henry stood outside and smiled. It was all going along the way it was supposed to. Even the bombing in the Hilton had worked out; Devereaux was now history and there was no one on Henry's trail. Unless Trevor Armstrong decided to turn him in and he couldn't do that without turning in himself. No. Everything had worked just fine.

Matthew O'Day came out of the gray-doored room and looked right into Henry's face.

"Like you said," he said.

"I'm a man of my word," Henry McGee said. "Have a nice trip, Matthew. And when you're in Chicago . . ."

"Yeah?"

"You know. Rattatat." He made a sudden machine-gun gesture. "Watch out for the gangsters."

FORTY-EIGHT

This is what had happened at the hotel before the bomb explosion.

Devereaux called Hanley from the lobby. He always used lobby telephones because of their anonymity and because it gave him a chance to survey his setting. The agent acts with suspicion so long that he develops a sense that everything at all times is suspicious.

It was early afternoon Thursday.

The telephone sounded at the other end and then Hanley's voice, so clear he might have been in the next room.

"I need authorization for some things. There are changes in the plan," Devereaux began.

Hanley said, "Miss Macklin. She would be there by now. I told her . . . your room. You're going to have to talk to her, Devereaux; she thinks you're in danger and she threatens Section.''

Devereaux said, ''What's the threat?''

''To tell things. If you're hurt.''

''I won't be hurt,'' Devereaux said. ''I'm a footstep behind Henry McGee and whatever is going down, it goes down in a matter of hours. I need some things. Ordnance.''

''What are you going to do? Start a war?''

''Complete a mission.''

''Mrs. Neumann is very upset.''

''She's paid to be upset. Someone has to have a conscience.''

''But not you.''

''No. I was paid all these years never to question certain things.''

''Where are you now?''

''In the lobby of the hotel.''

''Where's Henry McGee?''

''I don't know exactly. I do know who he's making contact with and I know—I think I know—something of the deal that has to be going down. Tomorrow. It'll go down tomorrow.''

''What kind of ordnance?''

And Devereaux described it exactly.

Rita Macklin cracked the pressed wood of the footboard and her legs were more or less free. But her arms were numb now and the headboard was much larger and that much harder to work against.

Sweat beaded her face and covered it with a fine sheen. Her eyes were desperate and something else they had not been for all the days since the bombing: they were alive.

She grunted beneath the sour dry taste of the gag across her mouth. The gag was tight and parted her lips and teeth and pressed her tongue down on the floor of her mouth. The gag also made it difficult to hear because it was pressed against her ears.

She pushed and pushed and she would never break this headboard. In her frustrated fury, she twisted around and her feet struck the floor at the side of the bed.

Leverage.

She stopped a moment to think about it. She tried to remember the principles from drawings in a high school textbook studied long ago.

She knelt on the floor and pushed her knees under the boxspring as far as they would go. Her arms felt as though they were being pulled out of their sockets. The tingling numbness extended back to her shoulders and burned across her back.

She pushed against the boxspring with her knees and pulled the headboard with her bonds and the pain almost knocked her out but now she felt something. The bed was shifting, confused by these two pressures on it. The bed was pulling away. An inch. Maybe two inches. Maybe a third inch. Each time she pulled at the headboard, she wanted to scream because of the pain but the dry gag stifled even that act of rage and frustration.

She pulled and pulled and pushed and pushed and now the bed was twisting itself sideways; the support of the broken footboard and rail was gone and the mattress and boxspring touched the floor on the foot end of the bed. The headboard began to bend against the underrails and she could feel another four inches and then the headboard made a terrible sound that was almost human and it collapsed against the mattress. Yes.

Yes. In her fury, her absolute certainty of the rightness of her hatred for the man who had tried to kill her and kill Devereaux, she was stronger than three men and the headboard bowed to her in honor of her strength. She got off her knees and dragged the headboard behind her to the door and she rubbed her back against the Plastique.

It fell from the doorframe onto the carpet, breaking the connection with the armed trigger in the doorjamb.

She kicked it away and then it was over and she fell, unconscious in her exhaustion, onto the remains of the bed strewn on the floor. She was still bound and gagged but she had done it and now the fury fell out of her in the obliteration of sleep.

This is the way Devereaux found her and the way Rita Macklin saved their lives.

FORTY-NINE

Dwyer was armed with an old-fashioned .45 Colt army automatic, the type of weapon called a horse-killer because it had been developed for the army after the turn of the century to allow the shooter to bring down a cavalry horse. Dwyer did not intend to bring down any horses today. He intended to get the boss's money back from Henry McGee, and if Henry McGee didn't like it, he would blow Henry McGee to kingdom come. And if Henry McGee did like it, Dwyer was going to do the same thing because you can't make a deal with a terrorist, not ever. The terrorist is a coward, Dwyer had told the boss, and like all cowards, he keeps coming back for more as soon as he thinks your back is turned. The thing to do, unless you want to cover your ass for the rest of your life, is to finish the threat once and for all.

Dwyer wore a light tan camel hair coat and a hat. He always

wore a hat. He was an old-fashioned kind of natty New York–type dresser who appreciates sharp creases, starched collars, diamond rings, and silk scarves. Dwyer had the great fortune of knowing exactly who he was and what he wanted to invent.

The boss was one hundred feet away, near the departure lounge, and he had a bag on his lap. Five million dollars in Swiss francs and British pounds and American dollars. It was a colorful payoff. Dwyer had helped him pack the case just as Dwyer had gone to the necessary banks in Belgium, France, Switzerland, and Luxembourg to get the money.

Him and the boss. Together. Just like at the beginning when he had hitched himself to the boss's star. Because Dwyer intended to be a rich man at fifty-five and take a very long retirement in the Caribbean, surrounded by beautiful black girls.

He saw the boss get up and walk across to Henry McGee and he saw Henry point to a third man. It had to be the terrorist, Matthew O'Day, who was shuffling along in the line that led to the jetway. The plane was boarding, as the loudspeaker said over and over. This was final boarding.

Henry McGee stood a moment with the boss and said something and the boss nodded and handed over the suitcase full of money. Dwyer pushed the safety on the horse-killer in his pocket. Henry McGee looked small and tough and Dwyer was small and tough and not afraid of anyone in the world.

Matthew O'Day settled down in the first-class seat and sighed. It was a pleasure to be away from the madness of the last two weeks. He buckled his seat belt and stared out the window. London was beginning to drizzle and the rain beaded on the thick glass that separated him from the rest of the world. The plane was filling, there were bumps and murmurs of "excuse me" in the narrow aisles and Matthew folded his hands over his belly. He closed his eyes. He thought he might just sleep his way across the Atlantic Ocean unless the movie was any good.

The baggage was loaded on a string of carts being tractored across the tarmac to the belly of the 747. Guard dogs had sniffed at the bags for drugs and anything else that might have threatened the safety of the flight. The dogs did not sniff the explosive plastic in the lining of the bag O'Day checked through because they had not been trained for that purpose.

Examination of the luggage, as usual, was cursory. The airline had not been warned to expect any terrorist act; the death of Flight 147 of a rival airline had not been forgotten but had been tucked away back in the collective memory in the corner reserved for remembrances of past acts of terror. It was just between the assassination of John Kennedy and the death of hundreds of marines in Beirut; somewhere in that area.

In a few moments, the airplane would lumber out to the runway and wait its turn in the line of planes heading for America and Asia. The foggy, rainy day of a little corner of the world would be shrugged off as the plane climbed through the clouds to the eternal clarity of the sky, where sunlight and moonlight are unfettered by mere weather.

And Matthew O'Day was already asleep, so that he did not hear the stewardess ask him if he wanted a cocktail before the flight began.

FIFTY

Trevor entered the limousine with his flesh-colored copy of the *Financial Times* tucked under his arm. He might be having a usual day. He said, "office," to the driver and opened the paper. The Rolls-Royce purred into drive and he began by burying himself in another of the interminable cycle of articles about the power of Europe after 1992 and what would pass for economic union in the Old World.

Dwyer would meet him back at the offices with bloody hands and five million dollars. Don't worry, Dwyer had said. Dwyer was as good as his word. Dwyer was as good as a dog. Funny he had never thought to name one of his dogs after Dwyer when he accorded that singular honor to his secretary. Funny. Because Jameson was today's driver.

These thoughts dimly filtered through his head. The car

picked its way through traffic around the airport to the M4 for London. The drizzle enhanced the closed feeling.

"Turn up the heat, Jameson," Trevor Armstrong said. His face was buried in the paper and his thoughts were on France and the French insistence that any united Europe would have France at its head. He shook his head. The French. They just didn't get it.

The automobile was picking up speed and something about this disturbed Trevor. The route to London was usually clogged. He looked up from the paper and looked around him and saw the wet, November farms of Middlesex streaming past the rain-beaded windows. Then he looked at the back of Jameson's head for the first time.

"Who are you?"

"Just the driver, lamb."

"Where's Jameson? What the hell is going on?"

"He was given the day off."

"Who the hell are you? I want you to stop the car—"

"On the M4? Do you want to get killed?" The chuckle was from the back of the throat. "Or maybe I shouldn't ask that question just now."

The traffic, murderous and pounding and very fast, created valleys of tire tracks in the flood of water on the roadway. Bleak November pressed at the windows and Trevor felt cold. The paper fell from his hands.

"I want you to stop the car," he said again.

"In a little while. We'll stop soon enough," Marie said. "I thought you wouldn't notice the driver. People don't. People like you. I thought about it but he wasn't so sure. I told him it would be all right because if you had noticed the driver, I would still have the gun."

"This is kidnapping—"

"If you were a kid. But it isn't. It's just a little ride into the countryside. A nice day for a ride to Oxford. Don't you think it's a nice day for a ride?"

Trevor summoned up his control. These things did not happen to people like him. Unless, of course, this was a final cross by the man called Henry McGee. Yes, that was it.

"I gave him the money. There's no point to this. He has all the money."

And he thought of Dwyer. What if there had been an arranged signal with some unknown confederate? And what if Dwyer managed to kill Henry McGee before the signal?

The clammy day had crawled into the car and was stroking him. He felt so very cold.

Dwyer felt the rain bake into his thick coat. The rain beaded on his hat brim. He watched Henry McGee cross the parking lot to his car. A remote parking lot was as good a place as any. He felt for the pistol in his pocket.

Heathrow was in mourning. The clouds yielded pitiful light rain, the kind that glazes roadways and makes all sorry creatures sodden refugees from God. The rain did not hush the rumble of traffic but made it seem more hideous because it was unrelenting when it should have ceased and waited for the clouds to part.

He did not even see the gray man until he felt the pistol barrel in his right ear.

He stood still. He knew exactly what this was. In 1957, he had felt a pistol barrel in his right ear while standing on a midnight platform of the Flushing elevated, waiting for a train to the city. He had offered a pistol barrel himself by way of explanation of his purpose three or four times in his life and he knew exactly how serious this was. They were between a red Ford Escort and a blue BMW and the world was all around them, rumbling and crowded, but they might have been the only creatures left on earth.

"Get in the blue car," the voice said. He could not clearly see the man until he was in the backseat of the car.

There was a red-haired girl at the wheel. The man with the pistol was gray, gray in eye and hair and face. He might have been the weather incarnate.

"This robbery?" Dwyer said.

"This is about your life," Devereaux said.

"What the hell do you want?"

"Do you have enough money? I mean, to retire on?"

"What the hell do you want?"

"Tell me about Trevor."

"I don't know what the hell you want."

"Open your mouth."

Dwyer looked at him. The man was murder without passion. Dwyer opened his lips and the man put the pistol on his tongue so that he could taste the astringency of the barrel. Dwyer absolutely understood and to hell with everything, he was no martyr; he had a chance to go to Vietnam when he was drafted and he bought an MOS to get out of it, five thousand bucks to the levy sergeant to get transferred to Fort Benning, Georgia, instead and clerk for an infantry company, better to sell weekend passes on the side as a clerk than get his fucking ass shot off in some fucking jungle somewhere with fucking assholes in black pajamas creeping around him. No sir, he was no martyr and the beautiful black girls who awaited him on Saint Martin had never been so far away.

"Whaddaya want?" But it came out garbled. That was because of the pistol in his mouth.

"I want to know everything. If I find out everything, you can live."

The red-haired girl looked at him across the back of the front seat. She was absolutely cold in her green eyes. She was as much death as this one. The death in them had filled the car to the temperature of freezing. Dwyer knew he was going to die and he didn't much care for the thought.

He made another strangled reply and the gray man took the pistol out of his mouth and put it between his eyes. He tried to see the pistol. He could see the hand of the stranger and see that the index finger was curled into the trigger guard.

"Boss was being set up. Extortion. Man wanted five million. Boss set up a deal."

"What was the deal?"

He was talking very fast, in case the gray man was in a hurry.

"Boss said to put the bomb on another plane. Man made the deal."

"What man?"

"Henry McGee."

"What plane?"

"Plane for Chicago. Takes off in ten minutes."

"And what were you going to do?"

"Get the money."

"Kill Henry McGee?"

"Jesus Christ. I don't wanna be set up."

"Nobody's going to set you up. You're going to become an honest man for a change. Trevor takes the fall."

"The boss?"

"Not anymore," Devereaux said.

"Kill him," Rita Macklin said.

"No. He can be useful."

"Kill him," she said.

Devereaux looked at her. "If you want me to."

Jesus Christ.

"Get the fuckin' bomb," Dwyer said. "Get the bomb off the plane. Get the fuckin' guy, this Irish guy that carried the bomb on the plane. Let him take the fall. Shit, let the boss take the fall, I give a shit."

"You're a loyal bastard."

"I don't wanna die," Dwyer said.

Devereaux looked at him closely as though he might be examining a butterfly pinned to a board.

"No," Devereaux said. "No one does."

Matthew O'Day opened his eyes.

The man in the aisle wore the expression of someone who knew everything and had seen everything. He didn't wear a uniform but Matthew could smell a man who was used to uniforms.

"Would you be kind enough to come this way, sir?"

Behind the man was the stewardess who had tried to wake him for a drink. He blinked. He looked out the window. He should have been thirty thousand feet in the air. He was still in the plastic cocoon of the aircraft and it was still parked on the tarmac, engines running to cool the interior. It seemed very cold.

"Sir?"

"Is there something wrong?"

"No, sir. Just a matter of some formalities," said the Englishman. He had a broad accent. Might have been Liverpool Irish. But this was crazy.

"I really don't understand."

And the large, moon-shaped face bent close. "Come this way, sir, we have to return to the terminal."

"Why?"

"There's the report of a bomb on the plane," the moon-faced man said. The eyes were hazel, without depth, barely opaque.

"I don't understand," Matthew O'Day said.

"It will all be made plain," the moon-faced man said.

FIFTY-ONE

Henry McGee parked the Peugeot in a no-parking zone on the side street off Maida Vale and walked down the block to the apartment building. The girls might be starting to stink but he thought he could stand the smell for a couple of hours of sleep. The flight to Tahiti wouldn't take off until 9:00 P.M.

The thing about it was how fucking easy it was, once you figured it out. Everyone expects to be given a pass; it comes with being alive and living on hope. Everyone figures that there are limits to cruelty and inhumanity when there aren't any. Everyone can be terrified because they don't really expect the worst thing to happen. Like Trevor. Like poor little Marie lying dead in the flat. Like Maureen, who was really a great lay. Like Devereaux and his girl friend. Like the whole fucking world that thinks everything is figured out and that terror is something you read about in *Time* magazine or something, something that happens to a bunch of ragheads in the Middle East or somewhere.

Henry had checked the money. If he was a man given to quibbling, he might have even counted it but it looked right, all those smiling and colorful Swiss francs with the money amount stamped out in plain English or German or whatever the fuck it was, the numbers were plain to see; and the pounds with the old queen ensuring that old Britain stood behind all this; and the dollars, the wonderful and small dollars with their quaint pictures of Capitol Hill and Independence Hall, dollar wasn't worth what it was in 1920 but what the hell, it was only money.

He turned the key in the lock to the flat.

This armed the trigger.

He heard the click and pushed the door.

This activated the trigger. The electrical charge went into the phosphorus bomb, which had been inert to that moment. The bomb was designed to stun and not kill. The only really evil thing about the bomb was the light.

The light was the light of a thousand suns exploding in a small room.

Henry McGee stumbled and fell before the light. The light filled the universe and was the beginning of matter or the end of matter; it was the last judgment in any case.

Henry felt his knees strike the floor and felt the bag fall from his fingers but, in that moment, he saw nothing at all. Heard the sound of the universe explode but did not feel it. Saw the whiteness of the world and the face of God.

He cried out. It might even have been a word.

FIFTY-TWO

Hanley said to Mrs. Neumann, "I think this is satisfactory."

"Yes. But I don't like it."

November smiled on the capital. The sunlight was bright and brittle and the shivering wind made everyone walk with quick steps and smile at being alive on such a day. God, that's the way Hanley felt. Bleak years and memories were shrugged off. He stood at the window in the corner office that looked down on Fourteenth Street and thought he had never felt so good. He might have two martinis for lunch, by God.

Only Mrs. Neumann sounded a note of gloom. Her voice was heavy and the weight on her shoulders had bowed them further. Each day, she was more and more bent until finally, someday, the weight of the world she lived in would crush her. Her husband saw it; those who loved her saw it; and none could do anything about it.

"Devereaux gave us an international conspiracy. He gave us a corporate head actually involved in terrorism. He gave us a solution, Mrs. Neumann, and he managed to do it with all the credit going to R Section. You can wear that credit when the budget is gone over with the National Security Adviser."

"But where is Henry McGee?"

"He's dead," Hanley said.

"Is he dead? I mean, where is the body?"

"A fire in that flat. They found a female body and they identified her finally through the IRA man they arrested on the plane. Maureen Kilkenny, shot in the chest. And Matthew O'Day, facing the rest of his life in Wormwood Scrubs. And Trevor Armstrong, indicted for conspiracy to commit mass murder. And—"

"But where is Henry McGee?"

"Henry McGee is dead. They found his body in the flat. Case closed."

"They were uncertain about the body, I read the scan."

Hanley just hated this woman at this moment. Her relentless gloom was beginning to infect his thoughts of lunch, of the giant cheeseburger with raw onion and the straight-up martini. Make that two martinis.

He turned from the window. "If Devereaux is satisfied, I'm satisfied. Case closed."

"And where is Devereaux? And Miss Macklin? Dr. Krueger is still hallucinating and now he says Devereaux impaled his hand on that spike."

"Nonsense. The man is a drug addict. I think that's been made clear."

Mrs. Neumann stared. She stared at the blank wall across from the windows. She stared into this world fabricated by bureaucracies and run by terror. She felt so very cold and bleak that she wondered if she might just kill herself.

"Hanley," she said.

Hanley stared at her and saw the weight on her and was moved to pity. He touched her shoulder, a thing he thought he would never do.

"It's all right," he said. "I know."

"They want to give him an award. November. They want to give him an award. The Security Adviser told us. A secret ceremony, of course. No names revealed. Just an award to be put in his two-oh-one file."

"I know," Hanley said, rubbing her shoulder to relieve her of the burden of office.

"An award," she said, staring at the wall.

And, inexplicably, she began to laugh.

And, just as inexplicably, so did Hanley.

FIFTY-THREE

C arl Greengold, who had once killed a man, sat behind the largest desk in the world and studied the dispatch. He had six young men in the room and everyone was devoted to him and his interests. New York screamed outside the window wall but he barely heard it. The continuous Dow ticker streamed across a second wall on a forty-foot-long lighted screen. The office was big enough so that the forty-foot-long screen still did not fill the second wall.

He had watched EAA for three weeks. Paper profits he had made had vanished as the airline tumbled down through the web of trades on the New York exchange. On paper, millions were gone. But Carl Greengold knew that paper was worth exactly what it was written on, no more or less.

The indictment of Trevor Armstrong and investigation of security lapses at the airline—the fact of the murder of four of Trevor Armstrong's household staff, previously hushed up, now revealed to be a plot by the Irish Republican Army terrorist, Matthew O'Day—well, it had made cowards of a lot of people who held EAA.

But not Carl Greengold.

He saw what the others did not see. There was an underlying value to the airline that mere rumor or even terrorism could not eradicate. The stock was around 40 at the moment—no, 39⅞ as it just trotted across the lighted screen—but there was no panic, no panic at all.

Carl Greengold looked up at Victor, one of his gang in the office.

"All right, Vic," he said. "It's down far enough. I want you to buy everything at thirty-nine you can put your hands on and do it as discreetly as possible."

"It won't last twenty-four hours," Victor said, speaking of discretion.

"I know," Carl Greengold said. "Thanks to our Irish Republican Army friends—even though they don't know it—I think I've just bought an airline."

Victor understood perfectly.

FIFTY-FOUR

"You killed him," Rita Macklin said.

He stared at the fireplace. Oak logs crackled. The gloom of a Virginia evening surrounded the cabin. It wasn't his own but a place he had purchased. In the spring, he would build a place of his own and spend his life raising timbers and making walls and stairs and rooms; he would fill out his life in this way. It would all be for her. It would be in her name and her soul, on deeds and on every record between them. He would marry her, he would court her, he would pledge himself to her, he would never lie to her and never leave her. He believed this.

"You killed him," she said again.

He looked at Rita Macklin, whom he loved. He stared into her green eyes, which had retrieved life. He rubbed her cheek with his fingertips and his gray eyes were full of life as well and not the empty, dead things they had always been. The eyes of the soul, he thought, a strange, poetic thought that he believed he had grown incapable of thinking. The eyes are the windows of the soul.

"I love you," he said.

"But you killed him." She had said this before, said it in the same, flat voice, like a child who wishes her parent to banish a dream of goblins and ghosts, to promise her that they will never die.

"Yes."

"You really did it. I can't believe you."

"Why?"

"Because it's so horrible. Because it's like someone telling me that they have finally stopped wars or that the bad things of the world are finally over."

"There is no Henry McGee," Devereaux said.

"There was. God, I still get nightmares. Is that what you had all those years? When you'd be sleeping next to me and then suddenly start speaking? You never screamed, you spoke."

"What did I say? You never told me."

"You would say things like, 'Yes, I'll kill you and then I'll kill your children.' Horrible things I couldn't believe. You would say things in such a clear, flat voice that I was afraid."

"Nightmares," he said.

"And now I have them too."

"I'm sorry," he said. He held her. They wore nightclothes because the cabin was cold despite the fire. She wore a flannel gown that could not be considered glamorous and he wore a large terry cloth robe that only hid his scarred body. Not glamorous and not at all sexy, either of them. Except they suddenly had an urgent need for each other and when they suddenly made love on the rug before the fire, when they moaned in delight and kissed each other to tears, it was not surprising at all. They were the only people in the world; they had finally found each other in the sharing of pain and in the sharing of the nightmares that now haunted both of them.

FIFTY-FIVE

Deborah Cummings, forty-one, a lawyer for the Justice Department who met a guy named Mac in a bar at the Willard Hotel in December and thought he was the most fantastic talker she had ever met and who also thought, like Mencken, that marriage was nine-tenths talk anyway, told her parents she was marrying this old geezer and they were as shocked as everyone else in the world, Mac included.

FIFTY-SIX

They were in Berlin again.

The day was clear and bright and Marie Dreiser had been shopping on the Ku'damm and she had been drinking a little too, with one of the boys she met in the hotel bar on the Panserstrasse. The boy wanted to go to bed with her, and who wouldn't, she looked better than she had ever looked, had even put on weight in the right places. That's what money did for you.

Devereaux had said she could only have a million dollars. Well, a million dollars was all right.

Devereaux had killed Dwyer and the red-haired girl didn't know anything about it. Dwyer had to die if the bargain was to be fulfilled because he was about the size and weight of Henry McGee. But Marie knew and that was all right too.

Devereaux and Marie had set the fire in the flat and the cops weren't too particular when they found the bodies.

"We're both killers, lamb," Marie had said to him.

"Just so you understand that," Devereaux had said.

"It doesn't matter to me, lamb."

The final act of terror had been played out just the way Devereaux had promised her in the flat that morning she had killed Maureen and saved his life. Terror for a life; revenge as a dish eaten cold. It was all right, everything was all right.

Marie knew she was a little drunk going home but that was all right too.

They had a lovely apartment and it suited her. She loved to hear the trains rumble on the elevated tracks at night. It reminded her of the little rat girl she had been in Berlin, living in basements and coal cellars, amidst the rubble of progress, grabbing a few crumbs of comfort from this one or that one, prostituting her body to save it.

She always wanted to remember because it kept her bitterness alive.

The driver of the cab took her change and bid her a good day and she opened the door and walked up the steps. She carried a package that contained silk underclothes and another that contained pâté de foie gras. She might have champagne tonight and pressed toast. She might do anything she wanted tonight.

She might let him make love to her.

She still liked that. She still liked that strong body filling her.

She entered the apartment and he stirred at the sound of her.

He was really beautiful, she thought.

"What time is it?" he said.

"What do you care? You're not concerned with time, are you, love?"

"I just asked," he said.

"Time I decided to come home. Did you clean the bathroom?"

He nodded at her.

She came to him and kissed him. He raised his lips to her. He wore a robe because he had no other clothes. He had not been out of this flat for three months. All of winter had enclosed them in the fastness of Berlin and he had wondered and schemed and tried to figure out what he could do but it was still beyond him. Prison had not been so unyielding to him; but this was a prison of soft touches and plenty of food and nights spent thinking of all the days when the images of life were around him.

Now there was only darkness. He had lived all of his life in sight and now there was nothing and he was a child in the womb again, aching to be born into the world.

But she would decide that. She decided everything.

Henry McGee remembered the last moment of sight, when he had pushed open the door of the flat and been greeted by a blinding light, the light of God or death, a light that had filled his eyes until they were blinded to lesser visions.

Blind.

A man even without clothing. A fugitive from the world hidden by a mad girl who controlled all of his universe. Could he call the police? This is Henry McGee, I am a murderer and wanted by a dozen countries. I am the man who killed all those people in Ireland. I am . . . what, exactly? Would prison be kinder for a blind man? Or would they kill him?

The problem was with killing himself. He could not do it. He had picked up a kitchen knife a hundred times and knew he could end it then but he could not. Too much of life remained in him to want to end his life. He hoped. He tried to figure a way. And he kissed his mad girl who was now only a sight remembered and was only touch and smell to him.

She kissed him again.

He wanted her, the life came to him again in a rush. He reached up for her to pull her face to his.

And she pulled back and he groped the darkness with his fingertips.

''Don't,'' she said. And she was laughing.

NOTE FROM
THE EDITOR

The story of Henry McGee can be found in earlier
books available from the publisher. They are: *Henry
McGee Is Not Dead* and *The Man Who Heard Too Much*.

The November Man chronicle has included the story
of Marie Dreiser in *The Man Who Heard Too Much*.

Rita Macklin has appeared in every book in the
chronicle except the first, *The November Man*.

The Irish Republican Army was first part of the
chronicle in *The November Man*.

ABOUT THE AUTHOR

An award-winning author and journalist, Bill Granger was born and raised in Chicago. He was a reporter, columnist, and critic for UPI, the *Chicago Sun-Times*, and the *Chicago Tribune* and still contributes regular essays to the *Tribune Sunday Magazine*. Twice nominated for a Pulitzer Prize, he has covered national and international stories, including the American race riots of the 1960s, the American Indian takeover of Alcatraz in the 1970s, and the civil war in Northern Ireland. His exclusive report on the role of a participant in the My Lai massacre won an Associated Press Award. His political reporting led to two books on Chicago politics—*Fighting Jane* and *Lords of the Last Machine* (with his wife, Lori Granger). Their book attacking special education, *The Magic Feather*, is still in print.

The November Man novels—twelve in all—were developed from Granger's experiences in Northern Ireland and in other travels abroad. His first police novel, *Public Murders*, won the Mystery Writers of America Edgar Award in 1981. *The November Man* (1979) attracted international attention because it seemed to parallel the real-life assassination of Lord Mountbatten, which occurred two weeks after publication. His novels have been translated into thirteen languages around the world.

Bill Granger served in the Army from 1963 to 1965. He lives in Chicago with his wife and son.